John Brunner

ENTRY TO ELSEWHEN

DAW BOOKS, INC.
DONALD A. WOLLHEIM, PUBLISHER

1301 Avenue of the Americas
New York, N. Y.   10019

COPYRIGHT ©, 1972, BY BRUNNER FACT & FICTION LTD.

ALL RIGHTS RESERVED.

COVER AND ILLUSTRATIONS BY JACK GAUGHAN.

Acknowledgments

Host Age first appeared in *New Worlds SF*, copyright 1955 by Nova Publications Ltd. First U.S. publication.

Lungfish first appeared in Britain in *Science Fantasy*, copyright 1957 by Nova Publications Ltd., and in the U.S. in *Fantastic Universe* (under the title *Rendezvous with Destiny*), copyright 1958 by King Size Publications Inc.

No Other Gods But Me first appeared in shorter and substantially different form (under the title *A Time to Rend*) in *Science Fantasy*, copyright 1956 by Nova Publications Ltd., and in its present form in *No Other Gods But Me* (Compact Books), copyright © 1966 by John Brunner. First U.S. publication.

All three stories have been completely revised by the author for the present book

FIRST PRINTING, OCTOBER 1972

3 4 5 6 7 8 9 10 11

PRINTED IN U.S.A.

Contents

HOST AGE 7

LUNGFISH 53

NO OTHER GODS BUT ME 91

HOST AGE

I

Cecil Clifford, staring down at the wasted face in which the old beauty was even yet discernible, at the dark hair spread across the pillow, waited a long moment before he could admit the truth to himself. His eyes suddenly began to sting with tears, and he blinked them back in anger. Tears could not wash away the fact of death.

At last he motioned the nurse to draw the sheet over the once-lovely face, and she did so. Turning away, he gathered up his instruments and found that the ward sister was eyeing him with a questioning but sympathetic gaze. He felt impelled to explain.

"She—she was the wife of one of my best friends," he said gruffly, and the sister gave an understanding nod. She made no protestation of regret, though, and he was grateful for that. His mourning was a very private matter.

And what had killed Leila Kent was a horribly public disease.

"If you'll make out the certificate," he concluded after a short pause, "I'll sign it before I go home."

He cast a final lingering glance at the still form on the bed, then moved heavily toward the next patient. There were sixty beds in this ward alone, each divided from the next by little folding screens, and every last one contained a victim of the Plague.

"There's only forty-seven for you to look at now, Doctor," he heard the sister say from behind him, and for a wild instant he could have believed that she meant he needed only to examine forty-seven more patients. Perhaps that day would come...

But she meant Number 47, Buehl, the spaceman, weak but recovering although he had gone ten days without treatment before his condition was identified. The Plague germ had been passing through one of its camouflage phases, and he had exhibited no symptoms worse than a bad cold. Until—*crash.*

Clifford wondered sourly whether the drugs and antibiotics he had given Buehl had actually had an effect. Apparently they had, for he was better. Yet he had tried the same combination on Leila Kent—and she was dead.

He shut the thought determinedly out of his mind. Still, the fact remained: Sometimes the Plague killed, about one in ten of its victims, regardless of what the doctors did, and at other times a therapy that had failed elsewhere would produce a miraculous cure in a matter of days.

Crazy! Crazy!

But the man in Bed 47 was grinning at him, and he had to force an answering smile for appearance's sake. "Well!" he exclaimed. "How's it going?"

The spaceman folded the technical magazine he had been reading and lay back, unzipping his jacket. "You might as well turn me loose," he grunted. "I feel fine. I could go straight back to space."

"That's for me to say, not you," Clifford countered with mock severity, raising his bronchoscope. Dutifully Buehl yawned to admit its tiny lamp and light-guide tube.

One glance, and Clifford knew he was right. He did not have to consult yesterday's picture of that inflamed throat to realize how nearly normal it had suddenly become. Tissues that a day ago had been swollen and an angry red were relaxing to a healthy pink. He shut the bronchoscope and confirmed his findings with his stethoscope. The breath that had rasped and gurgled in Buehl's lungs as though he were moribund from pneumonia now moved freely and almost silently.

Lucky bastard! Why him? Why not—?

Once more Clifford took a tight grip on his mind. There were other tests for him to carry out before he said anything. So far it seemed that anyone who recovered became permanently immune—a few brave volunteers had demonstrated that—but with a bug like this, versatile, unpredictable . . .

"Arm, please," he said, picking up the hemometer. Buehl peeled back his sleeve and let himself be pricked. The device clicked, and figures mounted the face of its dial: blood count normal, oxygen utilization normal. Watching him, Buehl chuckled.

"Trying not to believe me, Doc?" he demanded.

With sudden sharpness Clifford snapped, "Yes, you're on the mend! But one in ten of our patients dies whatever we do, and we want to find out what kept you alive but not them!"

Instantly sober, Buehl gave a nod. "I heard about that. And there are a hell of a lot of people with the Plague, right? You must be overloaded, putting men and women in the same ward like this." He gestured down the long room with its partitioning screens. "So you probably want to sample my blood, see if there's an antibody that turned the trick?"

"Yes, we'll be doing that," Clifford said, faintly ashamed of his outburst and covering his reaction by making a great business of sterilizing the hemometer probe. "So we have good reasons for not kicking you straight back to Mars."

Untangling the terminals of his portable EEG, he pressed down their suction-cup terminals on patches of shaved scalp hidden among Buehl's brown hair. "Eyes closed, please," he muttered, scanning the pattern that appeared on the machine's green-glowing screen. "Open—close . . . Right, keep them shut and think about something complicated."

"I've been reading an article in this magazine by a guy at Princeton. Says he's about to make spaceships obsolete. Will that do? He uses some pretty fierce math."

"That'll be fine," Clifford told him absently, concentrating on the EEG trace. Half a minute was enough to prove that Buehl's powers of intellection were back at their peak.

"You can relax," he said, and detached the terminals with a succession of little plopping sounds. Wryly he added, "I wouldn't have expected you to want spaceships to be consigned to the scrapyard."

"It's not a matter of wanting. It's more that I suspect the guy of being right. He might very well be able to build a matter transmitter."

Clifford glanced up, startled. "But I thought they'd proved that was impossible!"

"Oh, the old idea of scanning the molecular structure of something and piping it down a radio beam—that's definitely out. But this Professor Weissman is tackling it from another angle completely. He's talking about constraining one volume of space to congruency with another. Says if you managed that, an object introduced into one of the spaces would appear in the other as well. Sort of a macroapplication of the uncertainty principle. Say—uh—could you organize me the use of a computer terminal? I'd like to check his math."

Clifford blinked. He was well aware that even to be recruited into the space service one had to be outstanding in mathematics, but according to his record Buehl was only a midtechnician, and the idea of his correcting the work of a professor from the Institute of Advanced Study seemed improbable. Before he could stop himself, he said, "You really think you're up to it?"

"You mean healthwise? Oh, sure— No, that's not what you meant, is it?" Buehl gave a rueful grin. "Hell, that's what comes of being the hearty he-man type instead of a skinny, pale intellectual. Yes, Doc, I am up to it. I can run celestial mechanics in my head when I have to. Did have to once, when a pebble knocked out our nav computer on the Mars run."

Clifford gave an impressed nod. "Okay, I'll see what I can do. I don't know about letting you plug into the main computer—our statistics people have been screaming for lack of spare capacity—but would a regular portable calculator be any help?"

"Better than nothing," Buehl conceded.

"See that he gets what he wants, will you?" Clifford asked the sister. "And you can transfer him to a convalescent room now. He's doing fine."

So this bed can be assigned to a new patient, his mind ran on. *Buehl's quite right, we are overloaded—the Plague is eating up the country like a forest fire. . . .*

That completed his rounds for the afternoon, and he had never been so glad to finish a day's work. He had been on duty since six A.M., and it was now past four, and in ten short hours he had authorized the issue of nine death certificates—all from Plague.

Wearily he left the ward, stripping off mask and gown and sending them for destruction. Then he spent five minutes in the shower scrubbing himself with germicidal soap and reclaimed his own clothes from the ultraviolet irradiator where they had reposed since morning. By all accepted standards he was as clean as could be, but accepted standards had been going by the board with dismaying rapidity since the inception of the Plague.

When he entered the house surgeon's office to await the arrival of the death certificates, he found his night relief already there and on the point of going to scrub up. He summarized the condition of the more acute cases briefly, and they chatted in a desultory manner until the sister arrived with the documents from Records.

He was almost out on his feet by now, but determinedly he read through them all with care from sheer force of habit rather than because he expected to find any errors. He signed and thumbprinted them, then handed them back.

As she took them, the sister said hesitantly, "There's a policeman waiting outside, Doctor. Says he needs to speak to you personally."

"What the hell for?" Clifford snapped.

"He won't say. But he does insist that it's important."

"Oh, damn the man . . . Well, I suppose you'd better send him in."

He leaned back in his chair and shut his eyes. When he opened them again, a big fair man in inspector's uniform was standing in the doorway, wearing a harassed look that Clifford recognized; he had seen the same expression on his own features day in, day out, for the past several weeks.

"I know how busy you are, Doctor—" the newcomer began. Clifford cut him short.

"That's okay. Sit down. What can I do for you?"

"Thanks. Well, my name's Thackeray, Inspector Thackeray, and I'm with the Missing Persons department at the Yard, so I expect you can tell what I've called to see you about."

"I'm too tired for guessing games," Clifford sighed.

"Of course. I'm sorry. Well, you attended one of the first cases of the—uh—the Plague, didn't you? I don't know the official name for the disease."

"Nobody's had time to christen it yet. Plague's as good a name as any."

Thackeray nodded. "The case I'm referring to is that of an unidentified man who came into London by steam bus from Maidenhead. Swarthy, rather stout, aged between fifty and sixty. You know the one I mean?"

"Yes, I remember. He was unconscious when the bus reached the terminal and didn't speak again before he died. We've had several cases like that. I suppose our Records people notify your department automatically, do they?"

Thackeray scowled. "They do indeed. That's our problem. When you say there have been several such cases, you're understating the facts. There have been well over a hundred of them in Greater London up to now—people who were either hitchhiking and passed out in the vehicle or who failed to get out of a train or bus and were found to be in coma when someone tried to rouse them."

"A hundred? Sounds like a lot. But what can I do about it?"

"Half a minute, please." Thackeray raised his hand. "All the cases I'm talking about, regardless of age—or sex, come to that, because nearly half of them are women—have one thing in common. They weren't ordinary vagrants, who are few and far between nowadays. They were well dressed, and most of them carried large sums of money. But not one of them bore any sort of identification."

"That does sound odd," Clifford agreed.

"It's not just odd. I can assure you from my own experience that it's unheard-of. How many things does the average person carry which give the owner's name? Driving licence, credit cards, health card, insurance certificates, business cards, often personal letters. . . . At the very least we can find a laundry or dry-cleaner's mark. We normally dispose of ninety per cent of the missing-persons cases reported to us, even cases of genuine amnesia. The other ten per cent have excellent reasons of their own for disappearing and make a thorough job of it. They're escaping their debts, or a pregnant girl friend, or nagging parents. But I literally can't remember having run across a case with no identification, no clues at all, in the eight years I've spent with my department. Now, all of a sudden, we get a hundred within a few weeks!

"Well, we're not unnaturally worried. So it occurred to us to ask you, who have incidentally reported more of this type of case than any other doctor in London, whether you think the Plague could have deranged them to the point where they deliberately destroyed their identification."

He added apologetically, "If you think that sounds as though we're clutching at straws, you're quite right."

Clifford laughed without humor. "Inspector, I wouldn't be telling the truth if I said categorically it's out of the question. We don't know nearly enough about the Plague to say what it can and cannot do. All I dare say is this. Even though I've seen derangement result from Plague, it's been the sort of disorientation any fever-induced delirium entails. We have grounds for suspecting that in a handful of cases the consequences may be lasting, but we're still looking into that, and it's not my field, anyway."

He hesitated. "Even if I'd said yes, though, surely that wouldn't have solved your problem. Missing persons don't report themselves!"

Thackeray sighed heavily. "This bunch don't seem to have been missed by family or friends—that's what so weird! And we've been unable to trace any of them back further than the start of their last journey. Oh, we've turned up people who saw them waiting for trains and buses or even sold them a cup of tea, but no one who asked their names or where they'd come from last. And none of them regained consciousness in hospital."

"And you can't match them to any reports you have on file?"

"Not a single one. So we've started an intensive investigation in the area where they came from."

Clifford started. "You mean they all came from the same place?"

"Same general locality. All west of London, at any rate. Which might account for this hospital of yours having picked up so many of them, I suppose. But it hasn't helped us in the least to establish that fact; we track them back, and past a certain point we run into a blank wall." He spread his hands. "They might as well have dropped from nowhere."

Clifford hesitated. "As a matter of fact, that ties in with a suggestion that's being—well—noised around. You must have heard that this Plague is completely different from any other disease ever to hit us. Could the carriers quite literally have dropped from nowhere? I mean from space, without undergoing quarantine?"

Thackeray sighed. "Doctor, I'm surprised at you. I know there have been stories circulating, off and on for several years, about spacemen who successfully smuggled things back from the Moon, and if things, why not people? But believe me, it's not for nothing that Space Traffic Control adopted that unofficial motto of theirs."

"No sparrow shall fall?"

"Precisely. It can't be done! We work in close conjunction

with Customs and Immigration, naturally, because the easiest way for someone to vanish, even nowadays, is to go overseas, and I've been shown what their experts can do. Do you know what even a ground-based telescope can pick up at the orbit of the Moon—football, tennis ball, ping-pong ball?"

Clifford shook his head, fighting the urge to let his eyelids drift shut.

"An ordinary kid's marble," Thackeray said. "No bigger than my thumbnail. Next time someone tries to tell you about smuggling things from space, don't waste your time listening. And speaking of next times, if you ever get another Plague case in here, well dressed, with ready cash on him but with no identification, let us know at once, will you? You seem to be making progress all the time, and sooner or later one of them might recover enough to talk."

"I wish I was as optimistic as you," Clifford grunted. "But I'll make sure there's a standing order to that effect."

With profuse thanks and renewed apologies, Thackeray took his leave.

For another few minutes Clifford remained in his chair, brow furrowed. This was another mystery to add to the myriad that the Plague had posed in his own field. Its pathology was unreasonable; its response to therapy was baffling; and as for the causative organism. . . ! Not for nothing had they slapped on the tag *Bacterium mutabile*, "the fickle germ." There were plenty of organisms infectious to man with peculiar and elaborate life cycles: malaria, bilharzia, scores of others. But this damnable Plague was something else entirely.

At first, indeed, no one had realized they were dealing with a single epidemic; it was believed that fifty or a hundred had broken out at once. Sheer chance had led the researchers to the truth. One of the early victims happened to work in a dye factory—and turned orange as he died.

So now there was a test for the condition. Someone who at first sight might have seemed to be suffering from cerebrospinal meningitis . . . had Plague. Someone who might have caught the 'flu . . . had Plague. Someone who appeared to be dying of pneumonia . . . had Plague. There was no apparent limit to the variety of ways the bug could kill.

And yet it did not *always* kill. It went through quiescent phases for no detectable reason and was ignored because the symptoms were minor, could be ascribed to something commonplace, and disappeared when routine therapy was administered.

Over and above the ten per cent of the population who had

so far been identified as carriers in the areas so far affected—Greater London, part of the industrial Midlands around Birmingham, and the populous South Coast resorts—how many millions more were completely unaware of having been infected?

And what was the point of screening sixty million people when, even if you found the bug, you didn't know how to get rid of it?

Maybe we finally did it. Maybe our messing about with organic compounds finally cooked up a new life form that can kill us. . . .

But there were specialists working on that, and it was pointless to speculate.

Effortfully, he left the hospital and walked down the road to the park where he had left his little steamer. As he pressed his finger to the eye of its door lock, an electric news trolley rolled up and honked at him hopefully. The placards on its engine mounting said: PLAGUE—DEATH TOLL MOUNTS.

As though I need to learn that from the papers!

Ignored, the machine trundled off in search of a more promising client while Clifford slid into the driving seat. There he hesitated. He knew he needed to go home and get some rest. But even as he formulated the thought, he knew it was empty.

There was another obligation that lay upon him.

II

He parked facing a big sign that told the world that this was the home of Kent Pharmaceuticals, Limited. There was only one other car in the visitors' area, and despite his tiredness he stopped to admire it. He had always liked to look at fine engineering, and this was a brand-new Huntsman convertible, resplendent in scarlet, the finned cooling tubes of its recirculating double-expansion steam engine glistening along its elegantly sculpted flanks.

Hmm! One of those next time—if I'm lucky!

But he was wasting time, and tore himself away to enter the office block that faced the road. Kent Pharmaceuticals was a wealthy firm and less than ten years ago had rebuilt its entire premises, making them the most modern in the country. The spacious, almost arid reception hall was empty except for a receptionist who wore the haggard look characterizing anyone connected, no matter how remotely, with the heartbreaking fight against the Plague. She brightened slightly on recognizing Clifford.

"Good evening, Doctor," she said. "We haven't seen much of you lately. How have you been?"

"Busy as hell," he said shortly. "Is Ron in?"

"Yes, he is here. But at the moment he's showing a visitor around the labs. Someone from Balmforth Latimer, actually."

Clifford started. "Balmforth Latimer? Isn't that the village where they had the very first case of Plague?"

"That's right. He said he might have some new information which . . ." The girl's eyes searched his face, and she suddenly leaned forward. "Doctor, how's Mrs. Kent? Is it bad news?"

Oh, Christ. Does it show that much?

But there was no point in lying. Tiredly he said, "I'm afraid so. She died less than an hour ago."

"Oh, how terrible! Does—does Mr. Kent know?"

"The hospital must have called him by now. I . . ." Clifford had to swallow. "I just came to convey my regrets," he achieved, and thought what a sterile, shallow phrase he'd hit on. "Is this visitor likely to be long?"

"I don't know." The girl glanced around and tensed. "Oh— here he comes now!"

On the far side of the hall the door of Ron Kent's office was opening. A tall man with black hair lightly touched with gray came out, carefully pulling the door to behind him. He walked straight to the exit, barely according nods to the receptionist and the doorkeeper. He bore himself with a stiff, rather formal air; Clifford placed him as a retired soldier. Most of the armed forces of the world had been cut back in the past twenty years, and ex-officers frequently settled in quiet villages where their pensions would go farther than in cities.

The squawk box on the reception desk said something directionalized and incomprehensible, and the girl said, "Yes, Mr. Kent. But Dr. Clifford just arrived, and— Right away!"

Clifford, however, had not waited to be told and was already at the door of Ron's office.

There he was, seated at his desk, his red head bowed, his

thick-fingered hands folded together. He gave no sign of noticing as Clifford entered.

Awkwardly the latter cleared his throat. "You've heard the news, I suppose?" he ventured.

As though coming back from a great distance, Ron nodded, his head moving once fractionally back and forth.

"I just called by to say how sorry I am."

Forcing himself to raise his eyes, Ron said, "There's no need to tell me, Cliff. I know. Come in, sit down."

Clifford complied, and Ron went on. "I'd have liked to be there, you know. At the end." His tone was vaguely reproachful.

"Believe me, Ron, it wasn't possible. And in any case it wouldn't have been any good. We can never tell when a Plague case is going to go terminal. This morning, as I told you, Leila was doing fine. About noon coma set in. After that . . ." He shook his head.

"She'll have been cremated by now, I suppose," Ron said dully.

"I'm afraid so. Until we find out how to control the Plague, we have to take every possible precaution. After the case of that poor devil who worked at the mortuary in—"

He broke off, horrified at the way his tongue was jabbering away out of control, but Ron seemed not to have registered. He had picked up a pen and was turning it around and around in his stubby fingers.

"Nice of you to come, anyway, Cliff. I appreciate it. With the work load you're carrying, and—oh, *damnation!*"

The pen had snapped in half. He flung it furiously at a wastebasket. "God, I wish I'd stayed in practice instead of taking over the firm! I wish I could be *doing* something instead of sitting here and worrying myself out of my wits!"

"You're better off as you are," Clifford told him bitterly. "What do you imagine we *do*? Nothing! The Plague does as it damned well chooses! Oh, we save a few borderline cases, but we can't predict who'll live and who won't. I honestly couldn't swear that we've cured even one patient who wouldn't have got better of his own accord. In the last resort it'll be your people who find the answer. A doctor is as good as the researchers backing him up. We use the drugs, but you have to give them to us." He felt a need to get off this subject; it was too full of remembered frustration. "Who was that man I saw going out just now?" he asked abruptly.

"Oh, his name's Borghum." Ron rubbed his eyes with his fingertips, shook his head as though to clear it, and seized a cigar from a box on his desk. Biting off the end with repressed savagery, he went on. "He's from Balmforth Latimer. Remember the first Plague victim worked there as a gardener? Borghum used to hire him a couple of days a week."

"Did he have anything useful to tell you?"

"Of course not." Scornfully. "Didn't expect he would have. Though he used that as an excuse for getting himself shown over the labs. Well, it was a distraction, and that was welcome." Ron lit his cigar and spat smoke as though the taste was foul.

"A—a military man, is he?" Clifford said, desperate not to let the conversation die completely.

"How the hell should I know? I suppose so. He looks the officer type." With a shrug.

"Well . . . Well, did you have anything to tell him?" Clifford pressed. "Didn't you say something about a breakthrough when you called me up this morning? I was too busy to pay attention, I'm afraid, but I did get the impression . . ."

"Oh, you mean K39," Ron said. "Breakthrough is far too strong a word, but we are making a little progress, apparently." He tilted his chair back. "That's the chrysomycetin series, you know."

"Chrysomycetin? But I've used that myself, and it's given no better results than pantomycin, penicillin, or—"

"Tailored, tailored!" Ron interrupted. "You've met our head biochemist, Willie Jezzard? Well, a year ago he said he hoped to make a whole series of variants from it, five or ten times as many as there are penicillins, but it was too murderously expensive to give him what he wanted, so we shelved it until the Plague blew up. Now I've given him *carte blanche* and unlimited funds, and he's making headway. God, I wish I'd listened to him a year ago! It might have saved Leila!"

"Stop it!" Clifford rasped, half-rising.

For a long moment the two men locked eyes; then Ron gave a sigh and tapped the first ash from his cigar.

"I know," he muttered. "Spilt milk—stable door . . . Oh, forget it. I'll try to, as well. This is no time for weeping, is it? Particularly when we *have* made a real advance. K39 is showing something like thirty per cent inhibitory effect *in vitro,* and it's been stable for four or five days."

Clifford whistled. "That's amazing! I know from my own experience you can give the same drug to two Plague victims, and one will recover and the other won't, with no discernible difference between them. Sometimes I think I'm back at the witch-doctor stage, going through the motions and keeping my fingers crossed . . . But thirty per cent—yes, in a good many cases that could tip the balance, let the body's own defense mechanisms finish the job. Side effects?"

"Of course there are side effects," Ron grunted. "What do you think we're trying to eliminate? We don't even have to test it on a volunteer to know it entails a five-degree fever and generalized edema owing to increased cell permeability. But we do know one thing: It kills the Plague germ, and it need not *necessarily* kill the patient."

"Then why—?"

"Why haven't we announced the news? Use your head, man! Don't you realize we've been breeding *B. mutabile* for nearly three months and we still haven't found the repeat point in its adaptive cycle? Christ, it's like chasing an irrational decimal!" He uttered a wide swathe of pale-gray smoke. "Oh, that's a tough bug, that one. Every damned morning we have to burn out half our culture dishes. You know it can live off a medium which is ninety-five per cent its own waste products? It has a small-virus phase when it's effectively nothing but a naked gene, it has three large-virus phases that we know of, it has uncountable bacterial phases, and it has a pseudospore phase that it can go into from any of the others when it does nothing but bud off bits of itself and produces no symptoms! On top of that, it—"

"I know it's tough," Clifford said in a tone of deliberate mildness.

"Right. And we don't dare announce our findings for just that reason. For all we can tell it's totally adaptable. Some of the early samples went under to sulfanilamides. Now the bug will have a pint for breakfast and come back laughing. We thought we were on to something with scarlet fever antitoxin because it wiped out nine test samples in a row. The tenth time, not a goddamn thing."

"And it's still the same bug, not a laboratory mutation?"

"Hell, this thing *is* a mutation! Nonstop, in every generation! There's one giant molecule which codes its identity regardless of the shape it's in at the moment—and it goes through so many disguises it makes a liver fluke look like a bumbling amateur. That key molecule is resistant to almost anything short of poisons that would kill the patient, anyway. We can inactivate it with the dye test—you know about that, of course? That orange color signifies an irreversible change; the molecule is locked up for good, no doubt of it. But the dye also locks up hemoglobin and at least six essential human enzymes. What Willie Jezzard thinks he's got on to is a way of hanging a couple of *dextro*-groups where there ought to be *levo*-groups, and that screws the bug up because we're *levo*, for the most part, and— Hell, you don't want to hear me relaying third-hand data. I'm a chair-polishing administrator now and have been for years. Not even sure I could trust myself to bind up a sprained ankle any longer. Come down to the culture labs and hear it from the horse's mouth. If they could stand a visit from Borghum, they can stand one from you. You deserve it!"

III

The modernization scheme at Kent's had included the provision of all-remote handling for dangerous specimens, on the lines of the technique used for radioactive materials. They found Jezzard and his team of biologists—a girl and two young men—in a sealed room with one huge glass wall dividing it from the actual culture labs. From a solid bar running the length of this window, the intricately levered controls of surrogate hands dangled like enormous shiny metal spiders' legs, while the remaining walls were taken up with computer terminals, data-display screens, and a miscellany of equipment Clifford would not have dared to name.

Jezzard himself, whom Clifford had met previously, though only once, sat with his back to the airlock entrance poring over a stack of outline maps of Britain, identical but for the smears of blue chalk he had patched over them.

"Don't let us disturb you," Ron said as he entered. No one could have guessed from his tone or manner that he had lost his wife so shortly before. So long as the Plague could be reduced to the level of an intellectual challenge, there was a chance of obtaining unbiased results. Rather than regarding him as unfeeling, Clifford admired his self-control.

Jezzard raised his bespectacled face. "Back again, Ron?" he said, and then: "Oh, Clifford! What brings you here?"

For a second Clifford was surprised at being recognized;

then he recalled being told that the biochemist's great talent was for memorizing visual detail, and doubtless that included faces. He said after a brief pause, "I've just been hearing about K39. Is it on test at the moment?"

"We have a whole K series going," Jezzard answered with a vague wave in the direction of the glass wall. "Up to sixty-seven, actually . . . But you're right: K39 is the promising one."

He removed his glasses, wiped them very rapidly on the sleeve of his lab smock, and shoved them back on his nose, wriggling his ears vigorously to settle them. To the nearer of the young men, who was glued to the eyepiece of a remote viewer, he went on. "Phil, is it still cooking? This is Phil Spencer, by the way—Cecil Clifford."

The young man, tousle-haired and rather fatigued, answered in a guardedly optimistic tone. "Simmering, I think."

He withdrew from the viewer to make an entry on a computer reading while gesturing for Clifford to take his place. Bending to the binocularlike eyepiece, Clifford adjusted the focus until he saw the familiar outline of a Petri dish filled with pinkish nutrient medium on whose surface four smears of bacteria radiated at right angles from a central blob of pale golden crystals that he identified as pure chrysomycetin.

He manipulated the slide control, and the object glass slid along its rail beyond the window to the adjacent dish, then to another. In this 39 series there were nine altogether, each containing a different phase of the bug growing on a different supportive medium. Regardless of which phase was involved, although the *B. mutabile* had multiplied around the rim of the dishes, the spread was limited, and at the center there seemed to have been no reproduction at all.

Impressed, he relinquished the viewer to Spencer again. "Very promising!" he exclaimed, addressing Jezzard.

"There's one minor drawback," the latter answered sourly. "You've just seen nine-tenths of all the DDC in the world."

"Of the—what?"

"DDC! Di-dextro-chrysomycetin! That's what turns the trick, far as we can make out. The basic molecule has two levo-groups, and the bug not only tolerates them, it can actually make use of them. The *dextro*-groups put a kind of hammerlock on it, causing two of its template sections to weld together because they suddenly wind up facing inwards instead of outwards. But DDC doesn't occur in nature, and synthesizing it is the devil's own job. The yield rate is a quarter of one per cent at best, and separation is next to impossible! Still, it can be done, and as things stand, it will have to be. Because it's the only glimmer of light in this long dark tunnel we're groping down."

He stretched and gave a cavernous yawn.

"Matter of fact, Ron," he continued to his employer, "I'm glad you came by again. That guy you brought in earlier—the one from Balmforth Latimer—reminded me of an idea I've been meaning to try out. Know what these are?" He tapped his stack of duplicate maps.

"They look like the maps the Ministry of Health issue, charting the day-by-day spread of the Plague," Ron answered.

"Correct. But as you know, they only started to publish them about two and a half weeks ago, when there were already thousands of cases. This is the earliest." He held up one on which there were two patches of blue chalk, one large and centered on London, another smaller, centered on Birmingham.

"I've been having these scanned and recorded, and the computers should just about have finished analyzing the trends they indicate. Suppose we see what happens when you extrapolate those trends backwards, shall we?"

He pressed a switch, and on a small display screen that Clifford had not noticed on entering because it was adjacent to the door, a projection of the map appeared and began to change, with the crosshatched areas shrinking into clusters of dots that grew more and more isolated one from another until finally one was left.

Jezzard whistled. "I'll be damned!" he said. "I never expected to strike so close on the very first run! Look, that must be within—oh—less than ten miles of Balmforth Latimer."

Clifford said hazily, "Are you looking for a Typhoid Mary?"

"More or less," Jezzard agreed.

"Now just a second!" Ron exclaimed. "Looking for a carrier was one of the first things the ministry tried, and they decided that by the time the outbreak was general there were too many cases scattered over too wide an area—"

"Ah, but I'm not relying on the actual reports," Jezzard cut in. "What I'm doing is to extrapolate the later trend backwards, as I said. And there's the result." He pointed at the single remaining dot on the projected map. "Besides," he added, "who said it had to be a single carrier?"

"Think there's anything in this, Cliff?" Ron said doubtfully.

"Yes, I do," Clifford answered, recalling his encounter with Thackeray. "This ought to be passed to the ministry right away."

"Very well, I'll call them and get someone around to copy your data tapes," Ron said to Jezzard. "That is, if you've no objection."

With such a jerk of his head that he nearly dislodged his glasses, Jezzard said, "Lord! Do you think I'm worried about losing priority of publication? When we're faced with something totally new? You have to be joking!"

"Are you certain it's absolutely new?" Clifford demanded.

"Oh, it's so new it might well not have evolved on this planet. In fact, it very probably didn't."

There was a moment of blank silence. Clifford said at length, "But it can't have come from space. I have a spaceman in my ward right now, and I know how thorough his last quarantine was, and I was talking to a policeman this afternoon who—"

"I know, I know!" Jezzard said crossly, waving both hands as though to brush Clifford's words aside. "That wasn't what I meant. What I meant was, it very probably didn't *evolve*."

He glanced around with an air of defiance. "Well, work it out for yourselves. We haven't even been able to make this bug contagious between monkeys! Yet it's known to be infectious between humans. If it had—well—drifted down from space in spore form, you'd expect it to attack any kind of animal, wouldn't you? As things stand, we're having to grow it exclusively on human tissue cultures! Take that together with the fact that so far it's only appeared in Britain, and—"

"Are you trying to make out it's artificial?" Ron snapped. "And that it's being deliberately spread?"

"It's not such a ridiculous idea," Jezzard declared. "You know what the actual incidence is, don't you? Roughly one person in ten catches the Plague. Of that tenth, again one tenth dies. If that goes to completion we're going to lose one per cent of the population—six hundred thousand deaths! It's already started to paralyze the economy because even the people who don't die are ill for at least a month and unfit to work for twice as long."

"But for heaven's sake!" Ron exploded. "Who's the—the villain of the piece supposed to be?"

"I could make some enlightened guesses. We've lived in a troubled world the whole of this century. Knowing we've disarmed, demobilized most of our forces, an enemy could . . ." Jezzard's voice trailed away. He looked uneasily from one to another of his listeners.

With sudden authority Ron said, "Your job here is to find a cure for the Plague, not spread paranoid theories about it! I hope I hear no more of this. Cliff, we should be going; it's nearly five, and they'll want to clear up and get home."

Flushing, Jezzard said, "Don't include me in that. "I'm in no hurry to go. In fact I shan't be leaving until midnight, except maybe to have a meal."

"I thought it was Dilys's turn for the night watch," Ron countered, nodding toward the woman member of the group.

"So it is," she said without raising her head. "But I'll be glad of company."

"As you like," Ron sighed, and led Clifford out.

"Sorry about that," he muttered to Clifford as the airlock cycled. "Jezzard's our best man by a long way, but he does tend to nurse some crank opinions. He comes of an old naval family, I understand, and my company psychologist says he tries to regard the campaign against disease as a real crusade, fulfilling his unsatisfied longing for violence. The strain must be telling on him, I suppose. But as to the rest of his theory, it is infernally convincing, isn't it?"

Before Clifford could reply, there was a beep from Ron's pocket, and with a muttered apology he took out and spoke to a personal communication unit. After listening for half a minute, he pursed his lips and put it away.

"That's not such cheerful news," he grunted.

"What's happened now? Another outbreak?"

"Presumably. At any rate they've appealed to the World Health Organization to have Britain declared an Area of Menace."

"Have they, now! Well, that means we can call on all the emergency medical teams we need—"

"Yes, but think of the other side of the coin. No tourism, no business travel, no export trade, no space flights . . . You must know the provisions."

"I certainly do," Clifford said grimly. "It will make life tough for us. It must be the first time an entire country has gone under ban."

"A country as large as ours, certainly. Hmm! Glad I'm not going to be within earshot of Jezzard when he hears about this. It'll be grist to his mill and no mistake."

They were abreast of the door of his office again now, and halted, turning to face each other. Clifford was on the point of suggesting that they go out for dinner together, but a pang of pure, painful weariness reminded him that his duty to his patients must take precedence even over such a long-standing friendship. He and Ron Kent had met in medical school, had done postgraduate work in hospitals in the same group, and would very probably have gone into the next stage of their careers in parallel had not Ron's father died young and left him the chairmanship of the firm. He had been the best man at Ron's wedding to Leila . . .

Who is dead.

Before he had found the right words to excuse himself, though, Ron saved him the trouble. He said abruptly, "Why have you never got married, Cliff? Is it perhaps because you were afraid something like this might happen to you?"

He spun around and marched into the office, leaving Clifford staring somberly at polished wood.

No, he told the blank panels silently. *No, it wasn't that.*

IV

The shrilling of his bedside phone roused Clifford from deep, relaxed sleep. Thinking at first this must be the call he had ordered to wake him in time to reach the hospital by six, he stretched languidly. He had been in bed by nine last night and felt enormously better.

But as he turned over, his eye was caught by the luminous dial of his night clock, and he started. It was only half past three—much too early for his alarm call. He reached hastily for the receiver, preparing himself for an emergency.

It was one, but not of the kind he was accustomed to.

"Cliff, this is Ron Kent," the caller announced in a dead voice. "Listen, the police have just rung up from the works. Someone broke into the lab block, knocked out Jezzard, half-strangled Dilys Hobbs who was on night duty as you know, and just smashed everything to bits. Wrecked the whole K series beyond recovery."

Clifford's heart turned to lead. "Any idea who . . .?" he began, and words failed him.

"They've got a description out of Jezzard. Tall, dark, lean, no longer young but of athletic build . . . Sounds like this man Borghum, doesn't it?"

"Very like! And I know what a good memory Jezzard has for faces; after all, he recognized me this afternoon."

"Right. But the worst part of all is that Jezzard has told the police his theory about the Plague being spread deliberately."

"Are they taking him seriously?"

"Right now *I'm* half-inclined to take him seriously! Because the only alternative is to assume Jezzard went off his head and did it himself! And we dare not lose him! Look, the reason I'm calling you, I can't reach my receptionist—she's gone to her boyfriend's for the night or something—and I need someone who actually saw Borghum leave the premises. The police say the alarm systems haven't been tampered with, so they want to know whether he could have hidden somewhere in the building and then slipped away when the alarms were turned off to let the law in."

"I saw him go out," Clifford said. "Although of course he might have sneaked back in . . . Look, I tell you what. I've had plenty of rest, and I don't have to be on duty until six. Would it help if I came round to the labs?"

"Can you do that?" The gratitude in Ron's tone was almost pathetic. "When I think of all our work shot to hell, I feel I could kill the bastard who did it!"

His voice was on the edge of breaking. Clifford said reassuringly, "I'll be there as soon as I can. I'll see you in less than half an hour."

He did not bother to dress properly, but pulled on slacks and a jersey and ran down to his garage. At this time of night the streets were empty. Apart from a prowling police car that turned to follow him because he was exceeding the speed limit but fell back when he flashed his doctor's emergency light, he encountered no traffic until he reached Kent Pharmaceuticals. Here, there was chaotic activity. Four patrol cars were blocking the entrance; even what he recognized as Ron's own car had been excluded and was parked across the road. Men and women were milling around with cameras, recorders, and forensic equipment, while by the light of a hand-held floodlamp someone was assembling a Bloodhound—an electronic tracking device—on the tailgate of a van. A constable challenged him as he slowed the car, but on production of his identification he was allowed to enter the gate.

On foot, and after having his spoor sniffed by the Bloodhound to avoid possible confusion.

The echoing hallway, no more empty at night than by day but infinitely more cavernlike, was full of unprecedented noises: shouting, the whining of machinery, the stamp of feet. He cautiously opened the door of Ron's office and was greeted by a cry.

"Ah, thank goodness you're here!"

The occupants—Ron himself, Jezzard, the girl Dilys Hobbs, whom Clifford had met this afternoon, two constables, a sergeant, and a superintendent—all stared at him together. Jezzard's chin was bruised and had been smeared with some kind of salve, while the girl kept touching her throat as though it were sore.

The superintendent said, "Dr. Clifford? Come in, sit down. Ah—my name's Wentworth, by the way. Won't keep you a moment. Dr. Jezzard, you were about to say . . .?"

Alertly the sergeant held up the microphone of a tape recorder he was carrying on a sling over his shoulder. With the air of someone explaining the fundamentals of two plus two to a backward child, Jezzard recited his account of what had happened.

As he had said he meant to, he had remained in the lab along with Dilys Hobbs during the evening. He had been out for a meal at about nine and returned some fifty minutes later. The watchman had confirmation of this because he had had to turn off the alarms protecting the lab block and let him through. Then, at about midnight, Dr. Hobbs had gone to get coffee for both of them from a dispensing machine nearby. It had been his intention to drink it and then go home. When he heard the airlock door open, he had assumed she was coming back, but on looking around he had found himself confronted with Borghum, who punched him on the jaw and knocked him out.

When he came to, he found that the intruder had not only used the remote-handling mechanisms to smash all the culture dishes in the adjacent room but had doused them with a strong acid kept there in case it was ever necessary to destroy bacteria too malignant to expose to the outside air.

"It's such a senseless crime!" Dr. Hobbs burst out, her voice hoarse not only from emotion. Jezzard looked as though he might contradict her but thought better of it.

"And you?" Superintendent Wentworth grunted.

"I was at the coffee machine." A helpless gesture. "I felt myself seized around the neck and simply fainted." Another touch on her throat and a wince. "Whoever it was, he was an expert. He knew exactly where to find the carotid."

"But you didn't get a clear sight of him?"

Dr. Hobbs shook her head.

"And you, Dr. Clifford," Wentworth pursued, turning. "I gather you saw this man Borghum."

"Yes, a man was leaving the building just as I arrived this afternoon—last afternoon, I mean," Clifford said. "And I was told that was his name."

Wentworth rubbed his chin, it was stubbly with overnight beard. "I see. What brought you here, by the way?"

"I came to express my sympathy to Mr. Kent. His wife had just died in my hospital."

"I'm very sorry. I hadn't been told about that. Was it—uh —from Plague?"

"Yes."

"My condolences, also, Mr. Kent. As it happens, only last week my son . . . But never mind that. Dr. Clifford, give us your own description of this Borghum, please."

"About fifty, black-haired going gray at nape and temples. About six foot two or three, with a swarthy complexion and a pronounced hook to his nose. He might be Middle Eastern, Arabic or Israeli. He bore himself with a military air."

"And did you actually see him leave?"

"I saw him walk out of the main door, yes. And when I returned to my car a little before five, the one which had been parked next to it was no longer there."

"Ah. What kind of car?"

"A new Huntsman convertible in scarlet and chrome. I think the registration began with 9G, but I'm not sure."

"Good! Sergeant, see if you can punch for Central Vehicle Records from here, will you? Find out if there's a car matching the description registered in Borghum's name."

"Yes, sir," the sergeant said, and after a moment's thought dialed a long series of codes on one of Ron's desk phones. The others waited tensely. At length, having listened to a thin recorded voice, he put the phone down.

"Yes, sir. He does own a new Huntsman."

"Very well, put out a nationwide all-cars for it to be stopped if it's on a public road. And have the local police go to his home at Balmforth Latimer. It sounds as though he's our man."

"Shouldn't we wait for a check with the Bloodhound, sir?" the sergeant ventured.

"By the time they sort out the spoor he left this afternoon from the one he left tonight, he could be out of the country!"

"He couldn't, you know," Ron said.

"What?"

"We went under WHO ban at midnight. Didn't you hear about that?"

"No, I didn't!" Wentworth exclaimed. "I was asleep by then . . . Well, that's one thing in our favor—means he can't get away from Britain by air, not even in a private plane— But I'm committing the policeman's cardinal sin. I'm jumping to conclusions. I'd better do as you suggested, Sergeant, and see if they have that Bloodhound working yet."

Outside in the hallway again, Clifford turned to Ron, who was worriedly gazing at the procession of detectives going to and from the labs.

"What kind of an alarm system do you have here?"

"Not just *an* alarm system. We've got half a dozen interconnected. Not so much because we're afraid of being robbed as because some damned fool might break in and infect himself with a deadly culture. We always have a lot of fierce bugs around, you know. So the perimeter is covered with an electric-eye network, a sonar network, and a whole gang of pressure-sensitive wires buried just underground. Jezzard had to ask the night watchman to switch that lot off and let him through. If he hadn't, it would have raised hell from here to Hounslow. And before you ask whether Borghum could have slipped in at the same time, the answer's no. The movement of any warm object within the grounds is mapped by infrared detectors on a paper tape. We have the record of Jezzard's movements, so those detectors worked fine. And inside the building we have air-pressure alarms that react even if you open the door of a room."

"And no doors were opened?"

"Apart from the doors Jezzard had to pass through to reach the culture labs, no." Ron shook his head. "What it boils down to is that somehow this man got into the lab block without crossing the perimeter, burrowing from underground or dropping from the sky. Cliff, it's impossible!"

"If so," Clifford answered slowly, "you'd better call up your company psychologist and ask a few pertinent questions about Jezzard."

"You think— No, you can't think *he* did it! I only mentioned the idea on the spur of the moment because it was such a shock to be rung up and told about this in the small hours. But he's not crazy enough to ruin his own work!"

"I'm not saying he is," Clifford sighed. "It's just that I was watching him while he was making his statement. He's not so much angry about the damage. He's more angry at not having realized it was inevitable and taken steps to prevent it. That's an unsane attitude. It was neither foreseeable nor preventable. Who is your company psychologist?"

"We use a man called Chenelly." Ron was staring now. "Lord, I see what you mean. He did give that impression, didn't he? I'll take some precautions, then. He's been under terrible strain, like all of us, and if he actually breaks down . . . Thanks for the warning."

"Oh, you'd have noticed it yourself in a day or two." Clifford shot out his wrist to consult his watch and discovered he had left home in such a hurry he'd forgotten to put it on. "What's the time?"

"Ah . . . Nearly five."

"Splendid. I can go home and get dressed properly and still be on time at the hospital. I'll call you later, find out if there's any news. 'By."

He departed at a run.

V

He was thinking over that dialogue while he ate—or tried to eat—the tasteless stew that was the best they had been able to provide for lunch; one of the meat packers at Smithfield had died of Plague and the health inspectors had refused to allow the distribution of potentially contaminated meat. He had had to have it sent to the house surgeon's office. There had been three dozen new admissions during the morning, thirty-five Plague and the other appendicitis. The situation was rapidly approaching saturation point. If WHO didn't move in some trouble-shooters soon, there just wouldn't be enough doctors in Britain to cope.

Yet he found himself less concerned about that, which affected himself, than by Ron Kent's problem. How *could* a man have entered the burglar-proof premises of his firm?

Sounds like a job for Weissman's matter transmitter!

Well, it would be a handy explanation. Unfortunately this was still the age of spaceships relying on fallible rockets and long periods of coasting to drift them to the Moon or Mars. Matter transmitters remained a dream.

But . . .

"Oh, hell," he muttered, pushing aside his half-full plate. He was going to have to lay this ghost once for all. He pushed the intercom switch that connected him with the ward sister's office and, when she answered, said, "Sister, where did they put Buehl—the spaceman?"

"Ah . . . Ward 29. Why?"

"I think I'll just pop along and see how he is."

Walking briskly down the passage leading to the convalescent section, he wondered whether anyone had remembered to provide Buehl with the calculator he had asked for; he discovered on opening the door of his room that somebody had. He was making good use of it, punching figures into its keyboard with one hand while making notes on a scratchpad with the other. Glancing up, he broke into a grin.

"Ah, Dr. Clifford! Want to make sure I won't be troubling you again?"

Clifford forced a smile at the rather morbid joke. "As a matter of fact, I came to ask if you'd made any progress with that theory of Weissman's." And hoped Buehl wasn't going to ask why he was so interested.

"Oh, some," Buehl said, leaning back with a sigh. "This thing isn't worth a yard of comet's tail, not for a job on this scale. I could have done the lot in an hour if they'd let me plug into your main computer. Even so, I can tell you one thing. He's perfectly right."

Clifford was so startled he clenched his fists and took half a pace toward the bed. He said, "You mean he could actually make a matter transmitter?"

"Oh, no. Not a chance."

"I—I don't understand!"

"It's like the marble paradox. Ever hear of that? Fifty or sixty years ago, must have been, Banach and Tarski proved you could take a marble to pieces—five pieces, I think—and reassemble them to form a globe the size of the Earth. Conversely you could pack the Earth, properly divided, into a space the size of a marble. It's sound reasoning. The only hitch is, you just plain can't do it."

The magazine containing Weissman's article was open beside him; he tapped it with the pen he was holding. "Same thing applies here. He's quite right to say that if you could force two volumes of space to become totally congruent, something introduced into one would appear in the other. But in order to compare the identity of the two spaces you'd need to generate a signal that's flatly forbidden by everybody from Heisenberg on down. To start with—"

The communication unit in the pocket of Clifford's gown beeped and cleared its throat. "Dr. Clifford to the house surgeon's office, please, right away!"

Clifford muttered a few ripe curses. "Okay," he said. "Sorry to have bothered you." And turned to the door.

"No bother," Buehl said with a shrug. "But why the sudden interest in matter transmission? Is all this walking getting you down?"

With another forced smile, as false as the former, Clifford said, "Actually I'm trying to solve a burglary."

"Well, I tell you this straight," Buehl said with mock gravity. "If anybody had a matter transmitter right now, it wouldn't be a burglar. Someone that clever would choose a less risky kind of occupation. Like mine."

Making his way back to his office, Clifford was furious with himself for having taken the idea seriously even for a moment. Solving the break-in at Kent's was a job for the police.

It turned out to be the police who wanted him. In fact his visitor was a constable he vaguely remembered noticing outside Ron's office. Inviting him to sit down, he caught a look of surprise on the ward sister's face and wondered what explanations were being invented in the nurses' quarters for the law's sudden and repeated interest in him.

Tossing the plate of now-cold stew into a disposer, he said, "Okay, Officer, what's it all about?"

"Farquhar's the name, sir. I've been asked to advise you that we checked on the man Borghum, the one who was suspected of the damage at Kent Pharmaceuticals."

"And—?"

"The local police found him in bed when they called at his house this morning. It turns out that he had dinner with three friends at a restaurant last evening, more than a hundred miles from London, was seen to arrive about eight P.M. and didn't leave until midnight. Even in that Huntsman of his, it's out of the question for him to have got to London and back at the appropriate time."

"Then—" Clifford began, and broke off. It was no business of his to draw the police's attention to Jezzard's unstable condition. They might already have worked it out for themselves, anyway.

"Yes, sir?" Farquhar fixed him with bright, sharp eyes, making him feel like a specimen under a microscope.

"Then I suppose you'll have to start looking for somebody else," Clifford achieved with an effort.

"Yes, sir." In a deflationary tone. "Well, my super thinks it's best if the people who are—uh—in the know, so to speak, are warned right away not to repeat Dr. Jezzard's charges. Apparently Mr. Borghum was extremely angry."

He made to rise. Clifford checked him with a gesture. He had suddenly recalled what Farquhar had been doing last night—or rather, early today.

"Didn't I see you working on a Bloodhound at Kent's?"

"Well . . . Yes, sir. I've put in for CID, and you have to be acquainted with all the latest gear before you can pass the exams."

"Did it find anything? The Bloodhound, I mean."

Farquhar hesitated long enough to give himself away, and Clifford pounced.

"It did! What? A doubled spoor? In the culture labs, maybe?"

Farquhar looked extremely unhappy. Clifford added another wild guess.

"And didn't find a doubled spoor anywhere else! I'm right, aren't I?"

Farquhar yielded. "I've no idea what put you on to that, sir, but . . . Yes, that is what we found. We followed Borghum's characteristic aroma from the street, into Mr. Kent's office, and around the labs and back again. And just like you said, we found what seemed to be an overlay of much more recent spoor in that one area." He had the air of someone confessing that he had just found an untenable proposition in the creed he had followed since childhood.

"You mean the newer trace simply stopped dead? As though Borghum had vanished into thin air?"

"More or less, sir," Farquhar sighed, and added hastily, "Of course, you know, the Bloodhound is still experimental. Its evidence isn't admitted in a court of law."

"I'll be damned," Clifford said musingly. "Thank you, Officer. You've been very helpful."

"Thank *you*, sir," insisted the constable, plainly suspecting that something had gone obscurely wrong. He went out.

Completely baffled, Clifford spent the next several minutes

gazing at a blank wall. What the hell could you do with a puzzle like this one? Invoke a matter transmitter to solve it—get told with authority that such devices couldn't be built—and then discover that another gadget, also authoritative in its own way, required exactly that!

Oh, this is ridiculous!

No, those tamper-proof alarms at Kent's must have been circumvented somehow . . . and perhaps by this time the police had found out how. Instead of speculating pointlessly, he ought simply to telephone Ron.

But when he did so, he found there was no news apart from what Farquhar had just told him.

"Was the mess as bad as it looked?" he asked Ron.

"Even worse," the latter answered grimly. "We're probably going to have to repeat eight hundred and eight experiments."

"What? But you must have all your records, surely!"

"That's what I meant when I said the mess is even worse than it looked. The bastard spent a while working on our computer before he left."

"You mean the lab terminal isn't protected by an antiwipe code?"

"Of course it is, and only authorized personnel have access to it! Think I'm an idiot?" Ron's voice was harsh. "But when he found he couldn't expunge any of the data, he figured out an alternative. Oh, he's a clever devil, no doubt about it. There were some print-outs lying around the lab, the way there always are, and from those he must have got most of the addresses where we store K-series chrysomycetin data. So what he did was, he wrote in a new authorization code behind every last one of those addresses. Punch one, and what you get is a request for proof of your right to have the data printed out. And of course we haven't the least idea what answer to give!" Ron laughed half-hysterically. "Neat, isn't it? Of course the data are still physically there, but it could take us days or even weeks to sort them out!"

"Is anybody else working on tailored chrysomycetin?" Clifford asked after a pause.

"Oh, yes. Half a dozen firms. Far as I know, though, Jezzard is ahead of the competition by a mile . . . Are you wondering what I'm wondering?"

"Whether someone else may be due for a visit, too?"

"Exactly. But why, Cliff? *Why?* When it's the only hope we have of saving people from the Plague?"

A part of Clifford's mind that had been submerged for many years suddenly cried out. It was as though an aneurysm

34

had ruptured. Within the space of a second, he was helpless to reply in face of the recognition of how deeply he had been in love with Leila Kent.

Through a rush of black sorrow he heard Ron say something but had to ask for it to be repeated.

"You were right about Jezzard, I said!"

"How do you mean?"

"You've seen this morning's news, I suppose?"

"Not a chance. This lunch hour is the first free time I've had. People are turning up every few minutes—fresh cases of Plague."

"Well, it's not confined to Britain any longer. It's broken out on the Continent and in New York. Must be due to travelers who went abroad before they put us under ban."

"Oh my God," Clifford said slowly—and foolishly, he told himself. It was only what he ought to have expected. "But what does that have to do with Jezzard?"

"I told him about this, and he declared it was all lies, meant to distract attention from the fact that Britain is being attacked."

"Never!"

"I'm afraid so. I had to call in Chenelly, and Jezzard turned violent, and we had to sedate him. It may be months before he's fit to resume work."

"That's all we need," Clifford said disgustedly. "And there's going to be more of the same, you know. One of my nurses went into hysterics this morning, convinced she's got the Plague herself. No amount of negative tests can persuade her otherwise."

"I know how she feels," Ron muttered. "And that poor so-and-so Wentworth, who lost his son last week—he's being hauled over the coals because he put on that nationwide call to bring in Borghum, only to find he was a hundred miles away . . . Oh, the hell. Cliff, I have work to do, and so must you have. I'll call you at home this evening, okay?"

VI

More Plague cases continued to pile in throughout the rest of the day. By four o'clock every available bed was full, and he wasted another hour ringing the other hospitals with which they had exchange agreements, only to find the situation just as bad at all of them. Finally he had to ring the Ministry of Health and was told that as a rule of thumb cases obviously on the mend should be committed back to the care of their own doctors at home; extra home-nursing facilities were being organized.

It seemed like a last-ditch measure. He had witnessed so many unforeseeable relapses like Leila's. (Would he never get that out of his head: the beautiful wasted face, the dark hair spread on the pillow?) Some apparent convalescents might belong to the one per cent for whom nothing could be done.

Fatalistically, however, he complied with the order.

When he finally got away, he was more exhausted than the day before, and the next day promised to be even worse—and the next, and the next. He snatched a meal, and seven hours' sleep, and came straight back, to be met with the most cheering news he had heard in days. WHO had sent in a troubleshooting team from the American Midwest.

Their trucks, which he knew would have been driven ready-loaded straight on and straight off their globe-girdling six-engined transport planes, were being unpacked in the yard before the main entrance when he arrived back at four A.M.

He spent the next two hours touring the wards with a group of soft-spoken black doctors and nurses, none of whom seemed to have realized the true nature of the Plague before. That was hardly surprising, Clifford realized; up to now it had been contained within Britain. But he could see how shaken his companions were as he described in dispassionate detail the course of this most unpredictable of diseases. He asked them to diagnose the condition of one patient after another, and they produced prompt and should-have-been accurate answers: advanced bronchitis, kidney failure, inflammation of the pia mater, septicemia probably from an infected wound . . . and then had the accompanying nurses perform the quick, impressive test that turned a single cc of plasma, sputum, or urine that fearful, unique orange color.

Plague.

Still, the mere presence of these people was comforting. As in the body leukocytes gather to the site of an infection, so these experts had been whisked off their regular beat, flown across the Atlantic, and dropped straight into the middle of the worst-stricken area. It was an index of how much the modern world could do against its subtle enemies.

When they had finished their tour, they adjourned to Clifford's office. Looking around, he addressed their leader, a thin man called McCafferty with the scars of a thyroid operation on his neck.

"Well?" he said.

"Nasty," the black man answered succinctly. "Why didn't you scream for help before?"

Clifford shrugged. "I don't know. We certainly did leave it late. You know it's reached Europe and the States now?"

"Do we not!" said the prettiest of the nurses. "You're lucky to have got us, I'm telling you. The next call after yours was for Brooklyn. They just been hit with two hundred cases in a day!"

"That's not all," put in McCafferty. "Rumor says they've programmed fifty teams for China. They thought they had some new kind of influenza. Someone suddenly thought to run that test you been showing us, and it's Plague."

Clifford's heart sank. Even given the amazing efficiency of the Chinese medical system, which notoriously did more with fewer resources than any country in the West, that was terrifying news. It must have taken a long while before the proud Chinese brought themselves to appeal for help from abroad.

"Well, guess we'd better set to work," McCafferty said, and headed for the door.

Clifford's visions of day after day of unremitting toil had been forestalled for a while, at least. With the aid of the equipment that kept rolling in all day, the WHO team lightened the load on the regular staff by almost half. By noon they were coping with the flood of new admissions; by afternoon a field hospital had been set up in Hyde Park, and delivery wagons co-opted by the police as emergency ambulances were filling them with patients; by early evening computers were printing out shortest-journey routes for nurses to follow in order to make tours around the city and help harassed GPs sift out new Plague patients from those who had contracted more conventional disorders.

Somewhere in the middle of all this bustle Clifford found time to answer a phone call from Ron Kent, who was jubilant.

"Cliff, the most fantastic thing has happened! Ever hear of a woman called Sibyl Marsh?"

"Biochemist? Works at an American university?"

"Right! She's one of the finest biosynthesists in the world. And do you know what she's done? She called up an hour ago and had a long talk with Phil Spencer, and she says she's been tailoring chrysomycetin, too, and she's going to have her whole damned lab packed aboard a plane and come right over so she can combine her results with ours and maybe even start producing DDC in quantity!"

"But Jezzard said the yield—" Clifford began.

"She says she can get it up to about twenty or thirty per cent!" Ron exclaimed. "Oh, this is incredible! Wonderful!"

"Fantastic," Clifford agreed, and for the first time in days he allowed himself to remember what hope felt like.

The halcyon period lasted just forty-eight hours.

And then the flying lab was blown up.

One of the attendant biologists was dragged back from the flames that engulfed it shouting incoherently about there being a tall dark man in the plane, but when firemen fought their way in, they found nobody.

What they did find was the shell of a phosphorus grenade.

Clifford heard about that on an early news bulletin as he was dressing to go to the hospital. Panicking, he called his office to make sure no one had attacked the hospital and set the receiver down with his mouth in a grim line.

So someone was determined to prevent chrysomycetin's being used against the Plague. But who? And, above all, *why?*

The news reader had moved on to an account of Plague in Malaysia and Indonesia when the phone rang and he snatched it up again. It was an unfamiliar voice that asked, "Dr. Clifford?"

"Yes, who is it?"

"My name's Chenelly, Doctor. Company psychologist to Kent Pharmaceuticals and various other firms."

"Oh, yes. Ron Kent mentioned you to me."

"You were a friend of his, I understand."

Clifford caught at the verb. "Were? Has—has something happened to him?"

The solid floor seemed to have given way beneath his feet.

"I'm very sorry to be the one to break the news," Chenelly said. "But—yes, he died during the night."

"Oh my God," Clifford said, his palm sweating so much on

the instant he nearly lost his grip on the phone. "Was it Plague?"

"No, not Plague. He took poison."

There was a total silence, as though the universe had hesitated, uncertain what to do next.

At length Chenelly said, "I blame myself for not seeing he was at risk. I did notice how tense he was when I had to attend poor Dr. Jezzard the other day, but . . . Well, what tipped the balance was the destruction of the flying laboratory. You heard about that?"

"It—it was on the radio just now."

"Mr. Kent was told at once, of course. He had authorized the transfer to it of the entire remaining supply of this tailored chrysomycetin which seemed so promising. And I understand it has all been destroyed. He left a note in which he said this proved to him that someone is deliberately spreading the Plague—along the lines of what Dr. Jezzard has been saying. I'm afraid the note was very garbled, though."

Dead silence resumed. Chenelly said anxiously, "Are you still there, Dr. Clifford?"

"Yes—yes, I am." With immense effort. "Thank you very much for letting me know. Good-by."

But that, he told himself, was a conscious lie. He was no longer "still there." He was in a strange new universe where cold, inhuman monsters had taken from him first the woman who, all unknowingly, had prevented him from getting married, then his best friend, and now—or so it seemed—what might have saved the lives of countless others he had never met.

He sat down on the edge of his bed, put his head in his hands, and found that after twenty years of adulthood he could still weep like a little child.

VII

"Dr. Clifford?"

He looked up from a stack of case histories he had had sent

from Records in the vain hope of finding some new insight into the mutability of the Plague germ. "What is it, Sister?" he snapped at the woman in the doorway.

"You asked us to let you know if another patient came in well dressed but with no identification. We've just got one."

Clifford shuffled his papers together and jumped to his feet. "Where did he turn up?"

"Paddington Station, about an hour ago. We're trying oxygen, but he's very far gone." She added, "Dr. McCafferty's attending him."

Which was going to mean, Clifford told himself grimly, an argument. But things had now reached such a pass, any steps that might lead to a solution of this mystery must be taken, regardless of cost.

The new patient had been put in what had been a casualty reception room until it, too, had had to be turned over to Plague victims. McCafferty was bending over him, sounding his chest. He had the characteristically wasted face, and even from yards away Clifford could hear how his breath was rasping in his windpipe.

"Cliff, I don't get it," McCafferty said at his approach. "This guy should have been hospitalized a week ago, the state he's in. I don't see how he could stand up long enough to walk aboard a train!"

Clifford moved to his side, studying the patient intently. To the sister he said, "No identification?"

"None at all. He was carrying loose change, a five-pound note, and a single ticket to London. No wallet, no keys, not even a handkerchief."

"Which," McCafferty said with gallows humor, "you'd have expected him to need to keep his nose clear."

Clifford drew a deep breath. "Right. Call Scotland Yard, ask for Inspector Thackeray in the Missing Persons department—got that? Say we have one of his mystery cases here and he's to come around right away."

The sister nodded and hastened away to find a phone.

"What's all this about Scotland Yard?" McCafferty demanded.

"Think we can make this fellow talk?" Clifford replied obliquely.

"What?"

"You heard me!" Clifford snapped.

"Sure, but . . ." McCafferty licked his broad lips. "I guess we could—dry out his respiratory tract, give him a good fierce stimulant, maybe perfuse him with RPX— But hell, man! It'd cut his chance of survival in half!"

His black eyes fixed Clifford squarely. "I say you'd practically be signing his death warrant."

"I know," Clifford answered soberly. "But this Inspector Thackeray I just mentioned, he's been looking into the problem of more than a hundred people just like this one who've turned up unconscious with Plague but carrying no identification. And they all come from one area to the west of London. I think they're carriers. And I think they know it."

"What?" McCafferty's round head drew back like a chicken's on his scarred neck.

"Oh, I don't have any proof!" Clifford snapped. "But you know that Kent Pharmaceuticals had their lab wrecked? You know that flying lab was set on fire at London Airport? Doesn't it add up to the idea that someone's trying to make sure we don't cure the Plague?"

There was a tense pause. Finally McCafferty said, "Okay, Cliff. You've been fighting this bug for months. I just got here. But I think I've seen enough of what you're doing to believe you have a good reason. If it leads to consequences . . ." He hesitated. "Well, I'll share them with you. Fair enough?"

"More than fair," Clifford said, and thrust out his hand.

Forcing the stranger awake would be a tough task; they moved him into an operating theater to make sure the maximum number of emergency life-support systems would be on hand. While they were setting up their equipment, Thackeray arrived, and Clifford drew him aside to explain the risk they were running.

When he had finished, Thackeray said, "Well, I can take part of the load off your mind. We've already accepted the sabotage theory. That incident at the flying lab settled the matter. The home secretary has called a conference of chief constables for this afternoon, and the minister of health has sent an urgent memo to county medical officers. We heard about this because of course our department has the records on all the people who've turned up recently and can't be properly accounted for. Meaning, in practice, people like him." With a jerk of his thumb at the door of the operating theater. "What do you actually have to do to him?"

"Some very nasty things," Clifford grunted. "To start with, he can barely breathe; we're forcibly drying out his respiratory tract. To go on with, his nervous system is infested with the damned bug, and it— Oh, it'd take all day to explain just what it does to human nerves, but that's the commonest way it kills you. So we're going to perfuse his spinal canal—and his whole brain—with a stimulant called RPX. It's going to be rather as though the germ and the chemical are fighting to the death over control of his synapses. If he does respond, he may very well be delirious. But with luck we should be able to question him for about fifteen minutes and then flush his system out and leave him no worse off than he was before."

From beyond the door of the theater McCafferty called, "Ready when you are, Cliff!"

"Right," Clifford said. "Scrub up and put on a gown, Inspector, and we'll go on in."

"Can you hear me?" Clifford said to the man on the table. After almost ten minutes' work by McCafferty and the nurses, he had finally moved and put out his tongue to moisten his lips. His head had to be clamped because there was a perfusory tube in his neck, leaking a very dilute solution of RPX into his spinal canal, and for safety's sake Clifford had suggested having his hands and feet strapped down. It was not a position in which he himself would have cared to awaken.

But he thought of Ron and Leila Kent and kept reminding himself that this man might well be a mass murderer.

The eyes opened for an instant, took in the masked inverted faces overhead, the banked medical equipment. A sudden choking gasp, and they shut again.

Monitoring the patient's condition with an EEG, one of the nurses said sharply, "Doctor, look!"

Both Clifford and McCafferty turned to look at the machine's display screen. McCafferty whistled. "Hell, I've heard of that, but I've never seen it before! Cliff, I am right, aren't I?"

Clifford nodded in dismay. The traces on the screen were flattening literally as he watched.

"There's only one explanation. He's willing himself to die! And we've got to stop him! Nurse! Neoscop—ten cc's!"

The nurse had already begun to react and checked in midmovement.

"Ten? But, doctor—!"

"I said ten and I mean ten! *Hurry!*"

The nurse still hesitated, and Clifford, with an oath, reached for the drugs rack himself and charged a percutaneous syringe. He had never heard of anyone being given neoscop and RPX at the same time, but he suspected the results would be drastic, perhaps fatal.

And yet there was nothing else he could do.

He sent the dose into the man's carotid artery with deliberation, expecting with every second that passed that one of the others might shout at him to stop. They did not. And . . .

It worked.

Before he had withdrawn the syringe, the man's lips were writhing, and clear words—strongly accented, yet comprehensible—began to emerge. His eyes remained tightly shut.

"They cotch me! Die, die! Here now they are, we lost, we shall lose! Here now so far behind!"

Thackeray had clicked on a tape recorder, and every faint syllable was being trapped by the mike.

"So have failed, so have failed . . ." the man said in a tone of utter resignation. "Still, can die. Try to die. All is left . . ."

His pronounciation was curiously soft. He lisped his s's and all the shorter vowels were alike, and he said *uv* for "have" and *uh* for "are."

"Who are you?" Clifford barked. "What's your name?"

The man fought gallantly against the neoscop but had to yield. Licking his lips again, he muttered, "Name? Syon Famateus."

"What kind of name is that?" McCafferty demanded, but Clifford ignored him.

"Where are you from?"

"From? From—bomb—tom—tom-tom, tom-tom . . ."

"He's trying to escape into echolalic compulsion," McCafferty said suddenly. "What the hell could have scared him so much he'd rather be insane?"

There was an infinite weight of chill terror in the question.

Unexpectedly Thackeray said, "Syon Famateus! This is an order! Where are you from?"

"From-tom. Bomb-tom. Tom-tom drum-tum—"

"Answer me!"

And this time it worked. The man's face relaxed.

"Syon Famateus," he said in a near-normal tone. "Come f'om Pudalla in Taw City." It sounded like Taw City. "Um with uh sci'ntific divis'un uh th' adjust'ent caw."

Clifford, casting a worried glance at the screen of the EEG, which revealed that the man's strength was failing fast, tried to copy the authoritative ring of Thackeray's voice.

"Why are you here? What are your duties?"

"Mus' dissem'nate"—and the next word was a mere noise—"long's uh can. If uh'm co'ched by"—again the sound was incomprehensible—"mus' diet once." Alarm broke into the soft voice. "Co'ched! Co'ched! Mus' die. . .!"

He gave a sudden convulsion and went limp. The nurse at the EEG said, "Doctor, I have zero readings on all circuits."

"Yes," Clifford said, and peeled off his mask. "For all we could do, he managed what he wanted most. He died."

"But *why?*" McCafferty demanded when they had returned to Clifford's office. "I mean, I've heard about primitive people wishing themselves to death, but I never really believed it could be done. Yet I can't think of any other explanation for what this guy just did."

"I think," Clifford said softly, "that I could make a guess." And he added with a glance at Thackeray, "Can we hear your tape again, please?"

Shrugging, the policeman rewound it, and for the third time —once in the dead man's presence, once since they adjourned to this office, now again—they heard the breathy and mysterious words.

At the end Clifford said, "Would you agree with me that he was terrified of something so indescribably horrible he preferred death?"

"I . . ." McCafferty had to pause and think. "Yes, I'll accept that."

He leaned forward. "But the rest makes no sense at all! There isn't any place called Taw City! Not that I've ever heard of."

"He wasn't talking about a city," Clifford said. "That was just his pronunciation. You and I would call it 'Tau Ceti.'"

There was a dead pause. Then Thackeray exploded, "But damn it! Tau Ceti is a *star!*"

"Yes. I know."

"But . . . Oh, no. No, Doc. Sorry. I think I know what you're driving at. And I simply can't agree."

"Well, if you won't listen to me, maybe I can find you someone who can speak with more authority." Clifford touched his intercom. "Sister, that man Buehl—has he been sent home yet?"

"The spaceman?" the sister's voice replied. "Due for discharge today, I think . . . Yes, about ready to leave now. Want me to try and catch him?"

"Yes, please. Get him to my office at all costs—fast!" And Clifford turned back to his companions. "Now, listen. You heard this Syon Famateus say he was ordered to disseminate something. What's being disseminated here right now? The disease we know as Plague, correct?"

"Invasion from the stars?" Thackeray muttered. "No, it's

too far-fetched. Why, they're still arguing over whether it's worth sending a ship to Proxima, aren't they? And since we haven't yet been even to the nearest of all the stars—"

"*Yet*," Clifford said, and the point sank in.

"Cliff, are you crazy?" McCafferty snapped. "Star travel is hard enough to swallow without bringing in time travel as well! And, anyway, what conceivable reason could the future have for infecting its own past?"

"That I have no answer to so far," Clifford said. "But I think you're forgetting that we live in a four-dimensional continuum. If space travel— Yes?"

He had been interrupted by a knock at the door, and now it opened to reveal a very puzzled-looking Buehl.

"Doc, what's the matter? I was all set to go and relax in a nice luxy hotel for a bit, and . . ." His voice trailed away as he took in Thackeray's uniform, the tape recorder, McCafferty's stern face, Clifford's visible air of tension.

"I know, and I'm sorry," Clifford said. "But I have to convince these people—and probably a hell of a lot of others, too—that if you can travel instantaneously in space, you can travel in time as well."

"You're still hung up on this theory of Weissman's?" Buehl demanded. "I told you, it doesn't have any practical applications!"

"But if it did?" Clifford insisted.

"Oh, sure. If it *did*, of course you'd get time travel thrown in. It is time travel, in a way. If you cross space in nothing flat, you have to be moving back in time because light—C—is the limiting velocity. I guess you could rewrite the equations so that you started off at a later time than you arrived, like the young lady named Bright!"

"All right, let me put this to you," Clifford said, and leaned back in his chair and set his fingertips together. "When they took a Bloodhound around Kent Pharmaceuticals, they found the trace of a man they suspected of having smashed up the labs there. But they also found a much later spoor, which began and ended in the middle of the building. Behind not only solid walls but a whole gang of ultramodern alarms. And then when that flying lab was burned out, one of the people rescued said there was somebody else in the plane . . . who wasn't there when the firemen broke in. Both of these intruders match the description of a man who can prove he was a hundred miles away within a few minutes of being seen. Do I have to go on?"

Buehl looked puzzled. "Doc, are you saying somebody does have a matter transmitter?"

"Not does have. Will have. And are you going to contradict me?"

"I—I guess not. One of these days . . ." Buehl swallowed hard.

"Then what we have to do is set a trap," Clifford said. "With a hell of a lot of good sharp teeth!"

VIII

The culture rooms at the laboratory of Barnaby and Gloag, Limited were far less modern than those at Kent Pharmaceuticals, but that didn't matter. Barnaby's was a well-reputed firm with an excellent record of developing new antibiotics, perfectly adequate to support the well-publicized statement that they, too, were working on a tailored series of chrysomycetin derivatives. In fact they were not, but they had been offering for nearly five years a good strain of the natural product.

It ought to be convincing. Ought to . . .

Clifford stared with aching eyes at the dark mass of the sealed door dividing him from the culture lab proper. His hand was clenched around the butt of a pistol. Beside him Farquhar, adding yet another device to the long list of those he had to qualify on before being promoted to detective status, sat monitoring the unwavering luminous needle of an infrared detector that would instantly warn them of the materialization of a human being in the adjacent room. The whole building was infested with men and women waiting with guns and anesthetic gas sprays at the ready. Or supposedly at the ready. Even though Clifford had managed to argue the authorities into posting a watch here, nothing had happened last night or the night before, and if nothing happened tonight, the odds were that someone would say, "The hell with it!"

Unlikely though his hypothesis was, he remained convinced that it alone could account for the facts.

It was ten past two A.M. A dead time. His attention was wandering; he had been thinking about Ron and Leila, reviewing all the mistakes he had made.

There was a sudden gasp from Farquhar, and his hand slapped a master lighting switch. With reflex speed Clifford charged the door before him, all else forgotten. It had been disguised to look as though it was tightly sealed; in fact, it was set to open at a touch.

And there, in the center of the culture room, bathed in the pitiless glare of a dozen searchlamps, was a tall man with black hair going gray.

He looked wildly about as though to run, but there was nowhere to run to. Other doors vomited men with wire-rope nooses, who caught his arms and legs and dragged him away, heedless of how bruised the floor might make him. Anything to get him away from the spot that was congruent to the—the platform, the whatever, of his matter transmitter!

And within less than a minute he was safely removed to another room where something whined and something flashed and there was a prickling in the air and metal fillings in teeth ached at the very edge of pain. Everything they could imagine that might frustrate the operation of a transmitter was focused here; the space remained stable for no more than a millisecond at a time.

There, they released his bonds and allowed him to stand, and he rose to face the merciless gaze of those who had ambushed him.

"Aren't you going to will yourself to death?" Clifford demanded.

With curious dignity, Borghum shook his head. "That we only resort to when trapped by the Dori'ni." It was the word Famateus had used; the confusing sound was a kind of tongue click. "But how did you know of that, anyway? Did you torture one of my men?"

Clifford ignored the gibe. He said, staking all his hopes on this one sentence, "Where are you from—and *when?*"

Borghum stared at him with frank surprise. He said at last, "I would not have believed that you were open-minded enough to conceive the question. Since you are, I'll answer plainly. I was born here on Earth, but not until—let me see—what you would refer to as 2620 A.D."

"And did you bring the Plague to us?"

"Yes."

"But—but *why?*" Clifford took half a pace forward, fighting the urge to tear this dignified stranger limb from limb.

"Tell me one thing first," Borghum said, gazing at the gun Clifford held trained on him. "Is the Plague, as you call it, out of control beyond this age's ability to eliminate it?"

"Yes, damn you! Yes, it is!"

Incredibly, Borghum relaxed and gave a broad smile. "My task is done," he said simply. "Allow me to introduce myself. I am Colonel-General Andreas Al-Mutawakil Borghum, and I have the honor to be the commanding officer of the Corps of Temporal Adjustment of the Army of Man."

There was an instant of stunned silence. Clifford said foolishly at last, "So that's why . . . I mean, I realized you were a military man . . . But you haven't answered my question!"

"I can do so now, for I have nothing to lose even if you kill me. Everything it was possible for me to lose has already been swept into the abyss of an unrealized future." A few beads of sweat glistened on Borghum's high forehead, but his voice remained firm.

"I see that even if in this age you do not possess the techniques to build a matter transmitter, you are at least aware of how it can be frustrated." He nodded at the electronic equipment that was maintaining a constantly changing environment in the room. "I am glad you did not incorporate that in the burglar-alarm system at Kent's! Otherwise . . . No, I am getting ahead of myself.

"Bluntly, then: In the age from which I have returned we have established a chain of transmitters linking many of the nearer stars. We have more than a dozen colonies on other planets. Have? Will have? No, I should say *had*, for by my own actions I have changed the course of the history which led to them.

"What is important is that in the course of further exploration we made contact with an alien species, whom we know as the Dori'ni.

"In your terms they would have to be called psychotic. Believe me, we did nothing to antagonize them. On the contrary: We welcomed our meeting with them as the fulfilment of an age-old hope. We went to greet them in friendship, and they replied with an insane attack. Since they had the advantage of surprise, and since we had for centuries been accustomed to peaceful thinking, they drove us back to the few planets nearest Sol before we mustered forces to defend us.

"Yet we had one advantage. We had the transmitter, and they did not. We guarded that secret from them, even to the extent of hypnotizing our soldiers and ordering them to die voluntarily if they were taken captive. You know about this, I gather; I can't guess why, unless the man you questioned was deranged and believed himself to be on a Dori'ni planet instead of Earth.

"Of course the mere possession of a means of rapid transportation between the stars was not in itself a decisive factor. What counted was that the transmitter can be adapted to move objects, and people, *back in time*. The proof is that I am here, is it not?

"As a last resort, when we feared the Dori'ni would attack Earth itself, we established the Corps of Temporal Adjustment and set out to revise the history of all the battles we had fought in that dreadful war. I say as a last resort; naturally, using the transmitter for this purpose altered the whole of history, and I can only assume that in the alternate world where the decision was first taken we must have been completely desperate. After all . . . my corps exists!

"For a while we did turn the tide. But the final blow the Dori'ni leveled against us was too subtle, and too deadly. You must understand that for more than three hundred years no human being had fallen ill."

Bright and sharp, his gaze searched the faces of his disbelieving listeners.

"You find that incredible, don't you? But reflect a moment. By this time, on your local Moon, there are children who have never been exposed to the germs their parents knew. And we went on from the Moon, to Mars, to the moons of Jupiter, to the planets of other stars . . . and at each stage we left behind more and more of the organisms you tolerate because you are used to them. We developed means of identifying an infection within minutes of it starting to breed in the body; we were accustomed to carrying little culture tissues, programmed to identify and react against foreign organisms. To breathe on one, to swallow it, was a moment's absent-minded reflex—and the disease was cured!

"When the Dori'ni found this out, they built the Plague.

"No two cases of it are alike. It mutates according to the resistance it meets. The more frantically we fought it, the more efficiently it killed us. In your time one victim in ten dies. In my time . . . one victim in a hundred could hope to live!

"For we lost all the antibodies you carry as a matter of course. By the time you reach adulthood, you've won a victory over—how many diseases? A hundred, a thousand? Most of which you never even noticed!

"Whereas we died like—what was your vivid image? Ah! Like flies! And with the heartbreaking knowledge that the

Plague was the Dori'ni's last throw. But for that, we could have beaten them . . ."

He mopped his face, and his voice seemed to be near cracking.

"If we could have done so, we would have located the moment at which the Dori'ni infected us. But they were cunning. They gave the disease a long incubation period. Before we recognized it, literally a hundred million people had carried it through our interstellar chain of transmitters; it broke out so many different places at once, we with our shrunken resources had no hope of tracking it back to its beginning. You must understand that once I commanded half a million men and women. Do you know how many I brought back to your time? One hundred and fourteen!

"Yet I did bring them back, to carry out the most radical time adjustment of all, the only one which seemed to offer hope for the survival of mankind."

He bowed his head, and they had to strain to catch his ever-fainter words.

"We had to give you the Plague . . . for which there can never be a cure."

"What?" Clifford exclaimed.

"Why, yes. That's the whole point, don't you see?" A wheeze had entered Borghum's voice, as though he himself were on the point of collapse. "Do you think I'd have taken such pains to frustrate your experiments with chrysomycetin, had there not been an excellent reason? Until the bacterium had been made endemic, scattered so widely among the population that there was no hope of eliminating it entirely, I had to sabotage your most promising work. Now anyone and everyone will be exposed to it, forever—yet so many of you will survive!

"Out there, so far as the Dori'ni are concerned, all is as it was. When they meet us—fewer of us, perhaps, and at a later moment in time—they will once again launch their insane attacks. But by then we shall already have blunted their final weapon. I know that is so, for here I am, talking to you who are healthy still, who have doubtless been exposed, who have perhaps had it and dismissed it as a simple head cold! In each generation a few will die—a cruel choice. Yet its mere existence will ensure that medicine is not allowed to degenerate to a routine habit unsupported by original research and practical skills. That was what put us at the enemy's mercy. Therefore many who would have died will now be able to live."

After an eternal silence, Clifford said, "Why did you bring it to us first of all?"

"Because of your dense population combined with your many transportation links to the rest of the world. It seems we made a wise choice. For—"

The word was cut off by a sudden gasping cough, and Borghum fell headlong to the floor.

As Clifford knelt beside him, he opened his dark piercing eyes for the last time. He said, "You see? I who have benefited from the medicine of centuries ahead—I am dying! It was only an overdose that brought me here. I knew that if I could not return and take the antidote . . . ."

A rim of froth appeared on his thin lips, and he coughed again, louder and longer and with a fouler sound.

"But why didn't you reveal yourself? Appeal openly to us?" Clifford demanded.

"There—there are not only the Dori'ni out there. We had just discovered that. And we must not ever think of all of them as enemies. We— *Ach!*"

He convulsed in a final paroxysm and lay still.

There was a dull silence. At last Farquhar said, "Doctor, do you believe him?"

"I don't know," Clifford said. "But, like it or not, we're stuck with it."

He pushed through the others and walked, shoulders bowed, out into the cool night air. Overhead the stars shone down; from all sides he could hear the sounds of the city fighting its insidious antagonist, the howl of ambulance sirens, the whir of helicopters on errands of mercy, the muted multiple hum of countless engines.

He raised his head. Yonder in the darkness men and women were dying. Was it for a purpose? Did he believe Borghum's story? Would Ron and Leila have conceded that they had to die?

There would be no answer for a long time yet. Not until mankind came face to face with an enemy that might well not exist.

But if it did, then here, now, by himself and McCafferty and a million others, it was already being beaten.

LUNGFISH

I

Once upon a time there was a sea. It was full of life. It grew smaller and the life forms more numerous. There arose the problem of overcrowding. Perhaps, if any of the inhabitants had been capable of wonder, they would have turned their flat eyes upward and asked themselves what it was like above the sky, beyond the shining barrier of the surface. There was plenty of room there.

Eventually, some of them found out what it was like the hard way. Stranded by the tide, they gasped their lives away along the shore; dying, they left their outline in the mud, which dried, and was compressed, and became rock.

A billion years later, and many more than a billion miles away, a man was studying the fossil shapes of some of those remote ancestors.

The reflection seemed suddenly to telescope time, and Franz Yerring gasped. His hand shook as he switched off the projector casting images on his desk display screen.

For a long time after that he sat at the console and listened to the sounds of the ship, identifying every one of those that seeped through the thick insulating walls of the office with the certainty that came of having heard them over and over for thirty-seven years. He did not move except to breathe in deep, shuddering sighs until the buzzer on the door sounded. Then he roused himself to say, "Come in."

Tessa Lubova, his personal aide, slid the panel aside and stepped through with her habitual lithe grace. In her way she was beautiful, despite the remoteness of her expression, the mechanical calmness she shared with the rest of the Tripborn. She set the daily productivity reports before him without a word.

On the verge of leaving again, however, she paused and stared at him. "Is anything wrong?" she demanded. "You're very pale."

"It's nothing," Yerring said, rising stiffly to his feet. His voice bore an irritable edge that he did his best to disguise—it was not good to speak sharply to the Tripborn.

Tessa hesitated a moment, then shrugged with one shoulder and left the room.

Nice of her to notice, Yerring thought. *Most of the Tripborn wouldn't have done so. Or if they did, they wouldn't bother to comment.*

But then Tessa was one of the oldest of them.

He approached the multipanel on the far wall. It could be a picture, or an observation screen, or a mirror, according to whim. Selecting the mirror setting, he examined himself critically.

No wonder Tessa had been startled. He looked worn out.

Well, he must distract himself, then. He returned to the console, glad of the work she had just brought him. He had been trying to throw away time by studying that textfilm on paleontology, and had been unable to lose himself in it. No one in the ship could now escape the sense of tension that hung in the air like smoke. It had not been publicly announced that Trip's End was near—if anyone did know the exact time, it would be Sivachandra and possibly one or two of his navigation aides—but there were rumors.

And how reliable is a rumor? He posed the question wryly. He knew as well as any of the Earthborn why the length of the journey had had to be assessed with such a huge margin of error: not less than thirty-six, not more than forty years. From the remote Solar System it had been impossible to calculate with any precision how dense the dust clouds were that they must suck in for reaction mass. It was known only that there was plenty of dust along the route.

Still, they were finally within the likeliest target zone. Thirty-seven years, four months, and fifteen days.

It had been more like a segment of eternity.

He glanced at the summary on top of the sheaf of reports —square sheets of plastic that could be wiped and indefinitely reused—and gave a frown. Taking up a red write stick, he entered the day's returns on the screen of the master ecological chart that occupied one full wall of the office. On it, population was plotted against productivity: two curves, opposing and balancing each other, averaged out from dozens of past entries relating to air supply, vegetation, water reclamation.

It could all have been taken care of by machines. It had been judged better for the psychological health of the crew that it should not be. Daily, Franz had to review the data personally. He was glad of the fact. There were so few activities that lent meaning to his existence.

His frown remained as he mentally extended the current downward sweep of the productivity line. Either Trip's End was indeed close—

"Or," he said to the air, "we are going to be on short rations in less than a month."

That, he knew, was due to the sterile mutation in Culture *B. chlorella;* it had been dragging output down for days now. All the staff he could spare were busy tracking down the mutated plasm, and it was being steadily eradicated, but the job was a slow one, and each tank in turn had to be taken out of circuit, sifted, filtered . . .

"Hear this!" said the voice of George Hattus, ship's administration officer, from the public address speaker under the multipanel. "There will be a Captain's Conference at fourteen hours. That is all."

Franz took in the information automatically, his eyes still fixed on the down-trending curve. It was really a bad one this time. Not only did the *chlorella* cultures feed the crew; they were a key element in the recycling system. Perhaps he had recommended too great an increase in population on the strength of having got away for twenty years with no bad outbreaks of sterility. He should have allowed more margin for mutation due to the rise in radiation as they homed on the new sun that was their goal . . .

Just as well Magda has called this conference. Otherwise I'd have had to ask for one.

The wall chronometer showed that it lacked only eight minutes of fourteen hours. By force of habit he glanced around the room to make sure everything was in its proper place—it was—and went out, down the long green corridor toward the administration section.

Outside his own area of responsibility, the hydroponics section, he found a crew from maintenance taking up floor plates to get at a gravity coil that had been on the blink and called to the man directing the work.

"Captain's Conference, Hatcher! You heard the announcement?"

Quentin Hatcher merely looked at him with the strange cold eyes that all the Tripborn seemed to share and did no more than nod and stand back to let him pass. The rest of his team also glanced up; Franz could almost feel the chill of their gaze on his nape as he walked on.

I wonder when it first began. I wonder where we split in two.

Of course, like most of the Earthborn, he hadn't noticed it happening. Perhaps only the education staff had had the standard of comparison to judge it by. His life was shared with friends he had known for over forty years, ever since they came together to commit themselves as crew for a ship that then was no more than drawings on a board, stress equations in a computer, and a dream burning in a few men's minds.

But slow antagonism had arisen all about them, and the fact had to be faced. The Tripborn were—in some emotionless fashion of their own—resentful.

Or . . . No, perhaps it was not resentment. Perhaps it was something subtler. Scorn? For the Tripborn must be aware that it was with them that the future lay. The Earthborn were condemned to spend their lives in space, perhaps surviving long enough to see Earth again before they died—and perhaps not—while they, the Tripborn, would go on to plant the first human colony under an alien sun.

Once, long ago, he had envied them. Now he was no longer so sure about that.

Aside from a technician checking recording equipment,

there was only one person ahead of him in the conference room, and that was Tsien, the senior psychologist. He sat in his chair to the right of the captain's, bald head bent low over a stack of the ubiquitous reusable data sheets, examining psychometric graphs.

He nodded as Franz entered. And checked with a grunt of surprise. "Franz, what's the matter?" he demanded. "You look as if you've seen a ghost!"

Franz restrained the impulse to touch his face with his fingers, as though he could peel away the betraying expression he wore. He said wryly, taking his own place, "In a way I have. But don't let me interrupt you."

"You aren't interrupting. I've read these sheets a dozen times, and going over them again won't alter the facts they show. What is the trouble?"

Franz shrugged. "Oh . . . I was thinking about the size and duration of the universe. It was as though I'd had a vision of its full extent. It was—disturbing."

"I can imagine." Tsien settled back in his chair, big-shouldered, potbellied, reassuring of tone. "What made it so especially uncomfortable, though?"

"The sheer naked size of it!" Franz was astonished at his own vehemence and tried to continue in a calmer tone. "I mean, there I was thinking in terms of millions of years and how much can you or I hope to see? A hundred and twenty at best. That's the twinkle of an eye—"

"Wrong," Tsien shot back. "For us that's all the time there is, a lifetime. Beyond that, there's only numbers."

"Even so," Franz insisted doggedly, "we talk cheerfully about millions of years, we use words like 'age,' 'aeon,' 'gigayear' . . . And we have no gut conception of what they mean."

Tsien spread his hands, palms upward; the movement made his chest and shoulders heave like mountains in an earthquake. "Why should we? We don't have to survive a million years to think about them, any more than Sivachandra's team have to pace out the miles in order to measure the distance of a star. Think of yourself as measuring parallax, only by sighting on a fossil."

Franz started. "How did you know I was thinking about paleontology?"

"A guess," Tsien said frankly. "But a likely one. It's a symbol. We're here to make a new beginning, so we're drawn to reassure ourselves by studying other, earlier beginnings which we know led to successful outcomes. I've been doing the same, rereading pioneer papers about space neurosis. They're like maps that assure us we're not walking into unchartered darkness."

"But we are!"

"Not for the first time in human history. The circumstances may be new, but the process isn't. And another thing you ought to bear in mind. You were saying we can't take the long view—"

"I didn't say that!"

"You implied it," Tsien said firmly. "And you're wrong. This whole trip of ours contradicts the idea. Do you honestly think people like Garmisch, who conceived this ship, or Yoseida, who devoted his whole life to financing it and recruiting its crew, weren't capable of thinking beyond the limits of their own personal perceptions? Would you yourself have volunteered to come if you hadn't had a vision of millennia? It may be longer than that before the results are in, but we know they'll come. One day."

And then Tessa Lubova came in, silently, and instead of sitting beside Franz took a place, as usual, low on the left of the long table where the Tripborn members of Captain's Conference always sat together in a tight, exclusive knot.

This sort of thing is going to have to stop, Franz told himself, and on impulse called to her.

"Tessa, I'd like you up here next to me, please."

For an instant she fixed him with those stony eyes, and then she shook her head. Once. Quickly.

"I said—" Franz began, but Tsien laid a plump hand on his arm.

Under his breath the chief psychologist said, "No, Franz. It isn't something we planned for, this division. But we daren't deny that it exists."

II

One by one the rest of the twenty members of Conference took their places: Lola Kathodos of Engineering, Philippa

Vautry of Medical, Sivachandra of Navigation, the three Tripborn delegates apart from Tessa—Quentin Hatcher, Vera Hassan, and Fatima Shan . . .

There was a slight stir as George Hattus took his place on the left of the captain's chair. He was the most—how would you put it?—the most *unknown* person aboard. People tensed in his presence, though he was never anything but cordial.

Like a policeman rounding the corner, Franz thought, and remembered the days when there had been such people in his life. At sight of the familiar blue uniform, even the most law-abiding searched their consciences.

Yes, that's what George is. He's the ship's conscience.

Last of all, precisely on time, Magda Gomez took her place, and they all fell silent.

"Conference declared open," she said for the benefit of the record. "All right. Now I suppose you want to know why I've called you back so soon after our last meeting. It's because there are too many sanitation-type rumors going around about Trip's End. People have started to get sloppy and careless. I want it to be borne in mind that when we reach Tau Ceti II, our job will be *beginning*—not over and done with! We're here for a purpose, and we're going to carry it through."

Her gimlet eyes fixed on Sivachandra, and he looked uncomfortable; it was plain Magda had her own ideas as to who had let the rumors loose.

"All right, Siv, let's kill the guesses once for all. Tell them the date of Trip's End."

There was a rustle of excitement. Franz tensed. Sivachandra cleared his throat.

"We shall enter orbit around our target world," he said, "in about one hour less than fifteen days from now."

A babble of comment broke out; only the Tripborn sat as silent and immobile as they always did.

"Now that's out of the way," Magda said finally, "Lola, do you have a question?"

Lola Kathodos nodded vigorously. "Can we publicize this news or is it for our ears only? My section has been particularly full of 'inside information' and I'd like to squash it."

"Yes, by all means. And what's more I'm going to declare four hours' celebration time this evening. Mark you, I don't want anybody hung over tomorrow because that's when we get down to real work. Now we can put a bit of meaning into boat drill and landing routines. Hatcher!"

Quentin Hatcher cocked his head.

"The boat simulator is your responsibility, isn't it? I want you to pick your half-dozen best trainees and run them through a final test. Then Siv and I will decide who gets to make the first touchdown."

Expressionless as ever, Hatcher nodded.

"Before I move on to the next stage, does anyone else have anything to say—Medical, Administration, Psychology? Oh, Franz! Didn't Ecology have a report lined up?"

Not for the first time, Franz found himself admiring the way in which Magda kept her finger on the ship's multiple pulse. He spread his hands.

"To be honest, I was going to have to pass on some bad news, but the nearness of Trip's End solves the problem."

"Better tell us what it is, anyway."

"We've had a major attack of sterility in one of our most important cultures. Productivity is down in all areas—food, air, fresh water . . . Consumption would have been due to exceed output in a month or so. But by that time, I imagine, we'll be able to bring up raw materials from the planet and tide us over."

Magda glanced at Hattus. "George, what's the population right now?"

"Two thousand one hundred forty-nine," Hattus answered promptly. "It's one below schedule. There's a late birth coming up, isn't there, Philippa?"

"Yes," Philippa Vautry confirmed. "Edna Barsavitza is five days past due. I'll bring the labor on artificially; we won't want to deliver a baby while we're actually in orbit."

"So you think we don't need to worry about your problem, Franz?" Magda said.

"Not if we can bring up clean water and maybe some sterilized minerals from the planet," Franz agreed.

"Fine. Okay, Siv?"

"I think so," Sivachandra said after a brief hesitation. "You must realize that fifteen days' flight time may not sound like much compared with thirty-seven years, but we are making for a small planet rather close to its primary, you know, and until yesterday it was still around the limb of its sun. It's in clear sight now because we're in a braking curve, but so far we've been unable to do more than confirm that it's where, and more or less what, it ought to be. We've verified that the composition of the atmosphere hasn't changed since the survey robots came by—it's satisfactorily high in oxygen, that's definite—but after all, a whole century has passed, and the robots never actually brought us samples, only sent back signals.

"So tomorrow we'll be launching our spy-eye missiles in order to carry out a complete survey of the planet. Long before we reach orbit around it, we shall know what landing site will suit us best—"

"Are you landing party?" Vera Hassan said loudly from the far end of the table. There was sudden silence.

"What was the point of that, Vera?" Magda demanded in a voice like an Arctic wind.

"He said which site will suit *us* best." Vera leaned back in her chair, uncharacteristic defiance on her face. "But he's not one of the people it's going to *have* to suit whether they like it or not."

Franz gazed in astonishment. The other three Tripborn were nodding vigorous agreement, and that was something he had never seen before. Ordinarily they seemed immune to strong emotion.

What the hell . . . ?

But Magda cut the reaction short by slamming her palm on the table.

"Vera, you know perfectly well that Siv, or Franz, or I, or any of us, would change places with the landing party! But we can't! We're just . . ."

She hesitated and had to swallow before concluding in a lower tone, "We're just too old."

Too old! Those words echoed in Franz's mind. Too old even though scarcely two-thirds of his lifetime had gone by, because the remaining third was scheduled to be spent in this same ship, with nothing by way of compensation but the knowledge that he had contributed to making history . . .

He felt a sudden shiver traverse his spine.

What if I have nothing to show for it after all? What if— what if we fail . . . ?

Magda was still speaking, now in a more persuasive, in a coaxing tone. "Vera, all of us have dedicated our lives to an ideal, you know. The greatest task in history lies before us." She touched a switch set in the table top. "It lies right there!"

No one heard her last words clearly. They had all, even the Tripborn, turned to face the multipanel on the wall, which had sprung to life. It showed the disc of the reddish sun called Tau Ceti, set against a background of stars that were familiar to them all. But there was a new star among the rest: small, tinged with the same red as its parent.

Trip's End!

Franz heaved a slow sigh and stole a covert glance around

the group. The Earthborn were staring dreamy-eyed at their goal, except for Tsien, who seemed more interested in the reactions of his companions—but that was natural. The Tripborn, however, were sitting impassive, and once again Franz found himself wondering what their stony expressions could imply. Was it scorn? Was it contempt?

He couldn't tell, but he knew one thing. It might be—and it must not be—indifference . . .

Finally Magda broke the spell.

"That'll do for now. Remember what I said, won't you? Now go and inform your sections about the celebration time tonight. Conference adjourned at fourteen-nineteen."

She slumped back in her chair and added amid the shuffling of feet, "But I would like to see heads of departments in my office for a moment, please."

The pose of efficient domination that she had worn like a cloak at the Conference dropped off her the moment the door of her office slid shut. Indicating with a gesture that the others should sit down, she looked at Tsien.

"Well?"

The psychologist nodded. "I'm afraid certain—ah—steps will have to be taken, as we feared."

What was all this about? Franz glanced from one to the other of them. Magda noticed and rounded on him.

"Franz, what was your reaction to my little trick with the multipanel?"

"Why . . . Why, I didn't think of it as a trick. You mean you timed it so as to defuse Vera? There was a lot of tension, and she'd focused it."

"No, you're on the wrong track. The reason Tsien suggested I switch the view of Trip's End through to the conference room goes a lot deeper. Philippa?"

"The Tripborn!" Philippa said with vehemence. "How can they be so—so wooden?" Accusingly she stared at Tsien. "You ought to have foreseen it!"

"We did," the psychologist answered. "Or rather, Yoseida did. Given that a whole generation has grown up knowing no environment apart from the ship . . . George, we have sealed orders for use in this predicament. Get them out, would you?"

Hattus nodded and crossed to a safe set in the office bulkhead. From it he extracted a sheaf of envelopes with person-keyed seals, set to render the contents illegible if anyone but the addressee opened them, and handed the bundle to Magda.

"I myself," the latter said, "don't know what's in these envelopes. During one of the final briefings George and I attended before we left Earth, though, we were advised that emergency procedures would be made available if the psychological department deemed it necessary as we neared our destination. It's now more than a year since Tsien told me how concerned he was about the attitude of the Tripborn to the prospect of reaching Tau Ceti. So . . ." A shrug.

"I scarcely need to say this to you because you had the privilege of knowing Yoseida in person and working under his guidance before this ship was launched. But I do think it's plain that only a man who was completely devoted to the high ideal of spreading mankind through the galaxy could have visualized, so far in advance, the sort of all-embracing plan which I'm convinced we shall find in these envelopes."

There were nods from everybody. All of those present had indeed not only known but wholeheartedly admired that fanatical old Asiatic. Although it was not prescribed, they had developed the habit of meeting on the anniversary of his birth and sitting for a minute in silence before drinking a toast to his memory. He, far more than any other single person, had brought this noble project to fruition.

"We can't let Yoseida down now," Hattus said in his soft, agreeable voice. "We can build him no finer memorial than success in our enterprise. I suspect what's in these orders may not be very pleasant to enforce. But the least we owe to his memory is obedience."

Taking the envelopes back from Magda, he distributed them; the recipients eyed them curiously but as yet made no move to open them.

"Fifteen days isn't long to reorient over two thousand people," Tsien said thoughtfully. "The action recommended will no doubt be pretty drastic."

"Two thousand?" Philippa said indignantly. "There are nearly two hundred and fifty of us Earthborn, aren't there? And *we* don't need reorienting, believe me!"

"No, of course not," Tsien said in a soothing voice. Yet Franz had the impression he was annoyed with himself, as though he had made a slip and was covering up.

What sort of slip? Franz found he could not even make a guess. But the idea troubled him.

"Read your orders in your own offices," Magda said. "On no account let any of the Tripborn see them or even become aware that they exist. That's all. Good luck."

All except Hattus rose and went out. Franz contrived to follow Tsien into the corridor and drew him aside.

"Were you mistaken when you said you have to reorient all of us?" he murmured. "It seems ridiculous, but you sounded as though you meant it."

"And you don't think you need reorientation," Tsien said after a pause. "Very well, you're probably correct. But a little rededication may be required, if that's a more palatable term."

Franz shook his head uncomprehendingly.

Tsien sighed. "Think of it this way, Franz. In your office you have a multipanel, right? It can be a mirror, or a viewscreen, or a picture wall. There are thousands of the most beautiful views of Earth available for you to put on display—oceans, plains, mountain ranges, forests . . . But when did you last bother to switch one on?"

Dumfounded, Franz stared at him. "I . . . Well! To be honest, mostly I leave it blank."

"Exactly," Tsien said heavily, and walked on.

III

Franz returned to his own section with his mind in turmoil. Coming on top of the terror he had experienced when he wondered what it would be like to know he had wasted his life on a vain gamble, Tsien's last question had shaken him to his foundations.

He passed the envelope he had been given from hand to hand, impatient to gain the privacy of his office and find out what Yoseida had decreed as their final barrier against such failure. But before that he must announce the news of Trip's End to his own staff. Tessa, having returned before him, could have saved him the trouble, but he knew she would not have done so. Like all the Tripborn, she insisted with almost childish obstinacy that it was "not her place" to take on responsibility without being specifically ordered to.

What are they going to do without initiative?

Well, perhaps it would reappear under the stress of a

brand-new, unpredictable planet. Everything aboard the ship had to be predictable because otherwise it could not be secure. Doubtless initiative, original thinking, and enterprise had merely been inhibited by the environment.

He dared not let himself believe otherwise.

Tucking the envelope out of sight in an inner pocket, he stepped through a sliding door into the warm, slightly steamy air of the hydroponics section. Sometimes, looking down the lines of transparent culture tubes toward the blinding brightness of the light sources that fed energy into the vegetable reproduction cycle as might a surrogate sun, he was overcome with awe at the skill that had fined down the planet-sized ecological system of Earth and tucked it into the tiny hull of this ship.

Right now, though, he had no time for such self-indulgent thoughts.

Tessa was studying a sample of the mutated Culture B and at his approach said, not glancing up, "I suppose you want to address the hands?" There was, as ever, no discernible emotion either in her voice or in her features.

For a long moment before he answered, Franz gazed at her, thinking how little he knew of her personality, her affections, her likes and dislikes. He had begun the trip with a staff of twenty-one, whom he had met barely three years before departure, yet whom he had known as intimately as he knew himself. Now he had a staff of a hundred and three, all Tripborn except for him—because the new colonists must comprehend ecology above all other disciplines, his former hands had been transferred to shipside administration. He had known all his new staff literally since they were born: twenty years, twenty-five.

And yet he could not call one of them a friend.

At least, he comforted himself, *on the way back I can reclaim my old assistants.*

But what was he doing thinking about the return before the ship had even landed a scout, let alone the whole group of colonists? He shook his head, furious with himself, and strode onward, donning his dark glasses as he reached the big open platform between the tubes where dead cultures were slued for drying, lysis, and recycling to the organic intake pipe. There he halted, and one by one, without his having to call for them, the hands came to join him. Not talking, not betraying the least sign of excitement. Just arriving.

He tried to remember how he had pictured the enthusiasm that he had foreseen at Trip's End from the distance of thirty-seven years ago. He could not recapture what he had imagined; he knew only that it had been very different from this.

Don't they feel anything—don't they hope for anything? Are they human? Could they fall in love?

As children, they had been like any others. He knew that, for some of them were his . . . though he had never become a recognized "father" to any of them. The idea was that the whole of the Earthborn crew should stand *in loco parentis*.

And they had done so, tolerating their offspring when they were noisy, inquisitive, foolhardy, disobedient.

But that had been long ago. The children had grown into these frighteningly self-reliant teenagers and young adults who could certainly run the ship better than the Earthborn, yet they were devoid of imagination, initiative, ambition.

"Everybody's here," Tessa said, just loudly enough to break through his musing, and he made his announcement.

They took it as they took everything else, as though they were adding it to some store of information destined to be used in some calculation Franz could not even guess at. At their lack of response he boiled over.

"If only you knew how we envy you!" he exploded.

That, at least, took them aback. He rushed on: "You have your whole lives to look forward to on a good world, a new planet! We abandoned ours to make that possible, and I for one don't regret it—but I wish I could be your age again and take your place!"

He stumbled blindly away into the protection of a dark aisle between shoulder-high banks of culture tubes.

Someone was standing there, immobile. Franz was still wearing his dark glasses, and in the sudden shadow he could not tell who the other was until he had almost bumped into him. Then he realized it was Quentin Hatcher.

"What are you doing in this section?" he demanded gruffly.

"It is my free period," Hatcher said placidly. "I am having an affair with your aide Tessa. I came to see her."

His tone made it sound as though his own lovemaking involved no more of him than a bull would concede to one of a countless succession of cows. And, in a sense, that was what breeding had been reduced to aboard this ship. There was too small a genetic pool for it not to be systematically mixed.

"Very well," Franz grunted, and made to pass on, eager to gain his office and read his orders. But Hatcher prevented him: not by moving, but by not moving.

"Do you want something?" he rasped when the young man stood his ground.

"I have a question for you. You Earthborn are very free with your description of Tau Ceti II as a 'good world' "—Franz could hear the quotation marks. "Define, please, the standards by which you regard it as good."

"Don't be ridiculous," Franz snapped. "You probably know more about it than I do. Tessa does!"

"But Tessa"—the girl's voice came from behind him—"disagrees that the question is ridiculous. Is it that you have no answer we can understand?"

"Of course I do," Franz said, his nape prickling as he saw Tessa come around and take station at Hatcher's side. Their eyes, identically cold, were like the eyes of hostile judges at a nameless tribunal.

He drew a deep breath. "Look, do you honestly believe that if it were not an ideal world for colonization, we'd have sacrificed our lives to make your settlement there a reality? It's so nearly perfect, we barely believed the news when the robots signaled back the data they'd recorded. It would be like Earth itself if it had a large enough moon to cause significant tides! The sea is teeming with life, and much of it ought to be eatable—there's plenty of oxygen in the air because vegetation at least has occupied the coastal plains . . . Oh, compared to Mars, which didn't even have good air but which we settled nonetheless, this is a planetary paradise!"

"But it isn't Earth," Hatcher said.

"Some day it could be better than Earth," Franz said in a fervent tone.

"One is not excessively impressed by that," Tessa said, employing the increasingly frequent impersonal form that so many of the Tripborn favored, as though to sink individual identity into a uniform group. "You, after all, abandoned Earth."

"For your sake," Franz said. "In order to give you this virgin planet."

"And you say it's a potential paradise," Tessa murmured. "But if it isn't . . . ?"

Franz had been thinking of that risk entirely too recently for the question to be tolerable. He pushed between them and hastened away.

"It will be!" he threw over his shoulder. And as he drew out of earshot, he muttered, "It's got to be!"

Alone in his office, he sat down at his console and with

shaking hands groped in his pocket for the envelope of sealed orders. Panic surged as his fingers closed on nothing.

Then he felt in his other pocket and breathed a sigh: there it was.

Odd! I could have sworn I put it in the other.

But when he examined the seal, it showed no signs of tampering. He dismissed the momentary alarm from his mind.

Poised to rip it open, he found he was looking at the multipanel and recalled Tsien's recent question. How long was it since he switched an Earthside picture on? Years! It must literally be years!

And yet there had been so many scenes he'd liked in the enormous repertoire stored by the ship's master library—more, surely, than one could get bored with even after thirty-seven years. As Tsien had said, there were oceans and plains, forests and mountains, not to mention that fabulous view of Niagara, or the rioting foliage under Copernicus Dome on the Moon where he had spent his first vacation away from Earth as a small boy, stalking his father and older brother through the "jungle."

Most appropriate, thought, was one that brought an ache to his throat, he recalled it so vividly. It showed a panorama of wheat fields in North Africa. Only a century or two ago, the land had been desert; now it rolled for mile after yellow mile, every square yard bearing food for the benefit of mankind.

Yes, that was the right one to choose, now that a whole new planet loomed ahead.

He finally broke the seal on his envelope and found one sheet of paper inside. Closely typed, it ran:

Deliver at the captain's discretion to SENIOR ECOLOGIST. Greetings!

You will read this only after many years of travel. It is considered possible, though unlikely, by the psychologists who have mapped the predictable consequences of decades of isolation in space, that problems may arise as the time of ultimate planetfall draws near. Those who have been born on board may be reluctant to face the prospect of venturing out under open sky, no matter how hospitable Tau Ceti II may be to human beings.

As it has been explained to me, there is an analogy between leaving the ship and the process of birth. A child must relinquish the warmth and security of the womb. Those who have grown up in the starship must likewise be compelled to move to another stage of existence.

The following steps are to be taken to overcome any resistance they display.

(a) The senior medical officer will prepare a sufficient quantity of a drug that heightens suggestibility.

(b) The senior ecologist will select a means of administering it. Ideally it should be included in an item of diet that the personnel who must return to Earth can be warned to avoid. Aerosol administration that would affect all the crew equally must be avoided.

(c) In conjunction with the senior psychologist, who will organize certain alterations in shipside conditions designed to create subconscious discomfort in the minds of the landing party, the senior ecologist will render it impossible for the full complement of what I foresee to be roughly two thousand persons to remain indefinitely within the ship. If the guidelines laid down concerning rate of reproduction have been followed, there should be no need for actual sabotage, but this must be considered as a last resort.

In sum, even though shock treatment may be necessary, that landing party must be forced to leave the ship at all costs.

Franz's frown deepened and deepened as he read the document, and then at last he came to the signature. It was Yoseida's own!

Instantly all the doubts he had been entertaining vanished. It was as though the curtain of the past rolled back in his mind; once again he was a youth listening with fascination, with outright adoration, to that thin, sallow, fiery-eyed Japanese who was so set on sending mankind to the stars that he had devoted the whole of his colossal fortune to promoting the venture. Yoseida was the sort of man who could create loyalty with a single glance. In another age he might have conquered an empire or founded a great religion. As it was, he had welded together a commercial combine that united everything necessary for the launching of a starship, from mining to electronics, from printing to sewage purification.

When they built the ship itself, they found everything they needed ready to hand: that much smaller, that much more economical than life on a full-size planet actually demanded. So far had Yoseida thought it through.

The idealism he had felt then was still smouldering in Franz's mind, like embers beneath a heap of ashes. He clenched his fists with determination. In that moment he was more certain than he had ever been that they would not—they must not—fail!

His instinctive revulsion at the idea of deliberately making survival impossible aboard the ship had died as soon as he was aware of it. The overriding logic of the argument in the sealed orders had convinced him in an instant. He reached for his diet charts and studied them with care. An interesting problem, making the drug reach everyone it was intended for, without harming those who must continue to prefer the shipside environment because they would fly back to the Solar System once the colony was established. But there was a solution. He had known there must be one.

A far-sighted genius like Yoseida would never have set me an impossible task!

There was one minor drawback: He could not trust any present member of his staff to inject the drug into the diet converters. Since they were all Tripborn, they could not be expected to share Yoseida's vision. That would mean finding an excuse to visit the hydroponics section when everybody else was in Recreation, making the most of the allotted four hours of celebration time.

But an excuse could certainly be contrived. Doubtless, to the Tripborn, the behavior of the Earthborn must be as peculiar as theirs was to their seniors.

Their parents?

An ancient cliché occurred to him: generation gap! He almost laughed aloud. There could never have been a time in the whole history of mankind when it was more apt.

So now down to Medical, to see whether Philippa had the supply of drug ready yet. Rising, he made automatically to switch off his multipanel and checked his hand an inch before it reached its goal.

The panel was blank.

Yet, he could have sworn he had switched it on!

That, though, was a petty puzzle. He dismissed it from his mind and hastened from the room.

IV

Snatches of music from the recreation zone rang the length of the empty corridors as Franz walked circumspectly through semidarkness toward the diet-distribution room. At least the Tripborn were still human enough to enjoy singing and dancing, even though it made his spine crawl to hear their precise harmony, with never a wrong or overlong note, and watch their feet move in complex patterns as perfectly synchronized as if they were linked on unseen chains.

He was certain that this section of the ship would be deserted; nonetheless, he had rehearsed plenty of excuses to offer to anyone who found him here. Someone might overhear him from the sleeping quarters nearby, where his own staff were lodged, or someone might even have come for an unscheduled snack in the adjacent mess room. However, chances were that the music would drown out his footsteps.

All seemed peaceful as he drew the door of the diet room closed behind him. Like sleeping animals the looming food transformers awaited him in the gloom. The culture tubes produced only the most basic organic substances; *chlorella* could be eaten as it stood, but only in dire emergency could it be tolerated for long. These machines were what converted the algae into a vast range of nourishing, flavorsome, and substantial dishes. They filled the warm air with a rich and pleasant aroma.

He knew the layout too well to turn on extra lights. He crossed the floor swiftly, opening the additive caps on one transformer after another, and poured into each a careful measure of the reddish liquid he had brought with him in a jar. With the last transformer the jar was empty; he slipped it into a recycler for reduction to its elements and—confident of having completed his dangerous task in the secrecy that it demanded—returned to the corridor and walked away whistling.

In the humming warmth and dimness, Tessa Lubova emerged gracefully from the shadowed corner where she had been hiding. She made no attempt to discover what had been added to the food supply, nor did her face betray any hint of emotion whatsoever.

Resolution could be read in every face Franz looked at, and he knew the expression was matched by his own. He waited for Magda to speak up, and after a long delay she did.

"Phil, how about the suggestibility drug?"

"We took blood samples from random members of the crew," Philippa said. "Ostensibly they're to be included in the sampling chambers of the three spy eyes we plan to send to a soft landing—and of course they will be because we dare not let any of the Tripborn become suspicious. But we've run tests on them already, and they show just what we wanted. The incidence of the drug among the Tripborn is a hundred per cent."

Magda glanced at Franz. "Congratulations," she said with a nod. "I was worried for fear we might have to distribute a supplementary dose. Right, speaking of spy eyes: Siv, when can we expect the first remote pictures?"

"We've been lucky enough to approach at a period of minimal solar activity," Sivachandra said. "That means we shall have pictures by late this evening. Not of very good quality over this distance but stable and with adequate color registration."

"Fine. As soon as you can, plug them into the panels. Tsien wants to see what effect the sight of Trip's End has before he takes any—uh—any drastic steps."

The psychologist nodded heavily. "I'm still hoping that we may not have to take all the action we've prepared for," he said. "Because if we do, I'm not sure it can be managed. Not with so few of my staff to help me."

"How's that again?" said Lola Kathodos.

"Well . . ." Tsien licked his lips. "Well, obviously my Tripborn staff mustn't be allowed to guess what we're doing, and —oh, hell! To be frank, I'm not sure there aren't at least a few of my Earthborn aides who wouldn't let them know."

There was a sudden shocked silence.

Magda said at length, "Tsien, that's alarming. We've been taking it for granted that all the Earthborn are as determined as they were when we left Earth to see this project through to its conclusion."

A chorus of agreement broke out: "Yes, yes—of course we are!"

"Of course *you* are," Tsien said somberly. "But we, remember, are senior to the rest. We have been less exposed to— what shall I call it? To the apathy of the Tripborn, perhaps."

"Nonsense!" Magda said brusquely. "Franz here is as dedicated as he ever was, and he has no one but Tripborn staffing his section now. You're not losing heart, are you?" Fixing Franz sharply with her dark keen eyes.

"Of course not!" Franz exclaimed.

"So let's have no more of this defeatist talk, Tsien," the captain went on. "What is it that you think may be more than your trustworthy staff can cope with? Maybe we can help out."

"Possibly." Tsien sounded dubious but rallied obediently. "Well, we'll be using verbal suggestion, of course, starting rumors and scare stories, and there you certainly can be of assistance. I'll circulate a memo on how to deal with your subordinates, give you a list of weighted phrases and so forth. The rest, though, I'm afraid, requires specialized training. We'll be using subsonics, trigger odors, tactile suggestion . . . The idea, of course, is to invoke latent claustrophobia and make the environment of the ship intolerable."

"What if you don't succeed?" Sivachandra said, voicing the fear that Franz, and probably the others, dared not utter.

"Oh, it will work. I can assure you of that. Perhaps not by the time we reach orbit, but eventually." Tsien combed his sparse beard with his fingers. "My chief reservation is that we're having to use these techniques at all."

He hunched forward. "Consider! Every mass entertainment tape we've played during the voyage, every program of tuition in the schools, every talk, every briefing—the whole lot has been slanted toward planetside living. The inship systems were deliberately designed so that any average child could operate them by the age of ten. The rest of their thinking time—and the oldest Tripborn are in their middle twenties—was devoted to planetside studies. We've stifled every hint of exclusively shipside culture; we've identified and frustrated any child showing unusual intelligence or excessive talent for leadership. We had to, didn't we?"

So that's one of the reasons why the Tripborn are so uniform in their behavior! Franz started. Yet he saw the implacable logic that must have underlain the decision.

"Moreover we, the Earthborn, have deliberately made ourselves overweening. Authority in the ship reposes in *us*, not in *them*. We've held up Trip's End as a carrot in front of these conditioned donkeys—to use a crude analogy. It is there, and only there, that they can escape the restrictions we've put on them and achieve free and independent adulthood. By all the standard precepts the Tripborn ought to have absorbed a load of subconscious prejudices in favor of planetside life twice as strong as their inherent womb-retreat impulse."

"Should have!" Philippa echoed. "Must have! Why, we've even developed the easiest birthing methods in history to minimize neonatal trauma! Oh, we can't have gone wrong!"

"I think what Tsien is winding up to tell us," Franz said softly, "is that we have. Am I right?"

The psychologist admitted the charge with a nod. "Yes somewhere along the line this trip has altered our mental attitudes in a way for which there is no precedent. Franz, could it be because we're living in the first-ever closed subplanetary ecological unit?"

"No, it's not the first, even though it's the first to have to remain independent for so long. The early colonists on Mars similarly had to breed a new generation in artificial surroundings; it was over a century before the planet had been terraformed to the point where a child could walk under the sky, and even then he had to use an oxygen mask. It can't be as simple as that."

"Did we make a fundamental mistake by deciding to expand the population *en route?*" The question came from George Hattus, unexpectedly.

"We'd never have remained sane if we hadn't done so," Tsien said positively. "All the successful pioneering groups in history have included a wide assortment of age groups. Moreover, raising the children—which itself implied a new commitment to the future—occupied us during the most dangerous stage of the journey, the one which lay between boredom and fresh hope. I know all of us here have grown-up children. How many of us besides myself are grandparents?"

Hand after hand went up: Lola, Sivachandra, Magda, Hattus, Philippa—the last, to Franz's surprise, and she noticed.

"Didn't you know, Franz?" she asked cheerfully. "I'm sure I remember saying that I was going to stimulate delivery of Edna's kid."

Franz could no more react than a stone statue. Time seemed to have halted altogether.

But Tsien was saying irritably, "Never mind, we're all going to be grandparents soon! When we land, we can expand the population without foreseeable limit; Trip's End can easily accommodate a billion humans. Or maybe I should say: if we can land."

"If?" Magda echoed anxiously.

"This revulsion against landing which the Tripborn seem to display. It might be an inescapable consequence of their having been born in the ship. If so, human expansion to the stars will have to await the discovery of a faster-than-light drive."

"It better hadn't," Sivachandra said flatly. "To the best of our knowledge, that can never happen."

"And I'm dismayed to hear you talking like this," Magda

said in a determined tone. "We are not going to admit defeat, and that's final!"

"Hear, hear!" Franz exclaimed, and others echoed him.

"So you are to take all the steps laid down in your sealed orders, and if you need extra hands, you're to call on us." The captain was breathing heavily, nostrils wide. "Now let's turn to something more practical, shall we? Siv, you've organized your plans for the actual landing, right?"

"We're running pilot tests all the time. As soon as we hang up in orbit, we'll have a man or woman ready to go down. We've picked a short list of half a dozen; I'll delay my final choice until Tsien has given them all some final checks."

"Excellent. I think that's all, then, unless—Yes, Franz?" Struck by a sudden point, he had raised his hand.

"Philippa said the incidence of the drug has reached a hundred per cent of the Tripborn. But that's based on random sampling, isn't it?"

"Naturally," Philippa said with a frown. "We couldn't invent a reason for blood tests on everybody, you know."

"Well," Franz said doggedly, "suppose one of the Tripborn has in fact been missed out. Suppose one of them realizes the ship is deliberately being made uncomfortable?"

"Tell them it's because we're slowing to turn into planetary orbit and it's creating subsonic vibrations in the hull," Sivachandra offered. "Which is quite true. All of us are likely to feel ill at ease, aren't we, Tsien?"

The psychologist nodded. "It's as good a cover story as any. But if you do find someone who's missed the drug, get him to my department. Fast!"

There being no further business, they dispersed. In the passage Franz drew Sivachandra aside.

"I think you already know who's likeliest to make the landing," he murmured. "Why did you conceal the name?"

Sivachandra's pale brown face remained enigmatic. "I had reasons. You see, I have my eye on Felipe Vautry, Philippa's oldest son—"

And then it dawned on him, and his jaw dropped.

"And yours?" he forced out.

"Yes," Franz agreed. "But don't get upset about it. I didn't even know he'd made me a grandfather. Siv, something's wrong. Something has gone abominably wrong!"

V

And yet . . .

No, perhaps he had been mistaken. Perhaps things had not gone wrong after all; perhaps they had gone right in the curious, twisted fashion that was all that life aboard the starship would permit. There could be no such thing as "a home" within the ship; the whole of it had to be home for everyone. From the distant standpoint of Earth there had been no way of predicting that the original crew members would survive. It would therefore have been risky to encourage the kind of attachment to a narrow family group that was the custom on safe, hospitable Earth. Franz had sired three children: Felipe and two daughters. He had not complained when he was required to commit them to the crèche and then to the ship's school. They were by three different mothers, after all. From the beginning he had regarded them as due to be dropped, like pieces of a jigsaw puzzle, into those spaces within the ship that were precisely the right shape to receive them.

After that they were simply . . . Tripborn.

I don't even remember how old Felipe is! Twenty-four? No, he must be twenty-six!

And here was another Tripborn: Tessa, whose parents he did not know, and perhaps she didn't know, either. And he was supposed to be discussing a course of action with her.

"Now we have to prepare to jump either of two ways," he said in a strained, uncharacteristic voice. "Which we pick depends on whether the spy eyes spot an ideal location for the settlement. You have heard that they're going to relay pictures direct from the planet this evening, haven't you?"

Silence.

"Tessa!"

The girl's sullen face turned toward him.

"You weren't listening!" he accused.

"But I was," she said in her unchangingly calm voice.

"Then why didn't you—well—even nod?"

"Oh, I wasn't listening to you," she said, with that overtone that he had so often tried to label: scorn, contempt, indifference . . . "I was listening to the ship."

"What about the ship?" Franz hoped that the sudden guarded alertness in his manner didn't give him away. "It's bound to be making funny noises. Remember we're slowing to fall into planetary orbit. It was much the same when we were accelerating away from Sol," he added glibly, thinking that if he must tell a lie it might as well be a good one. He had no way of determining whether she believed him, but he ploughed on.

"Suppose you pay attention to me for once, hm? We're getting into a damned dangerous situation, you know! Our margin for error is dropping like a stone. As things stand, our resources will last about two weeks past the point at which we enter orbit. If we can land a hundred people straight away, that'll lighten the burden enough to get us by. Otherwise we're going to have to import raw material from the planet."

He reached out and turned on the multipanel, choosing a view of some Martian plantations. It had just occurred to him that they would provide an object lesson. Mars had been an infinitely worse planet than the one they were now approaching; visual proof that it could be tamed and rendered habitable ought to influence the Tripborn usefully. He was surprised that Tsien hadn't thought of expoiting the idea.

Rapidly he ran down the arrangements that had to be made to meet either contingency and finished, "Sound out the rest of the staff for their opinions, please. Sivachandra will pick the site of the first landing, but it must be you who decide where to locate the actual colony. After all, you're going to live there." He had to make a conscious effort to avoid saying, "You'll *have* to live there."

"Is that all?" Tessa asked.

"For the moment, yes."

She rose with her usual fluid grace and went out. Franz waited until she had closed the door, then switched the multipanel to remote viewing, anxious not to miss the first of the pictures that shortly were scheduled to be relayed from Trip's End. He had been staring at the blankly luminous surface of the panel for fully fifteen seconds before he realized it had been just as blank before.

What the hell happened to that picture of Mars?

He pulled out from the bottom drawer of his console the picture-setting index that he had not bothered to consult, believing that he had long ago memorized the code numbers of all his favorite scenes. When he had checked twice to make absolutely sure, he leaned back and drew a deep breath.

No wonder Tsien hadn't thought of using that picture of Mars to encourage the enthusiasm of the Tripborn.

There was nothing remotely similar in the list.

But I'm sure I saw it! I saw it as clearly as I saw . . .

And then he remembered that when he had picked out the

view of the North African grain fields, he had never actually switched it on.

Badly frightened, he rose blindly to his feet and walked down the corridor toward the mess. He needed a chance to relax, have a drink, talk about something else. Just as he reached the entrance, Hattus's voice echoed from the PA speakers.

"Hear this! We are receiving the first clear pictures from our spy eyes!"

All else forgotten on the instant, he rushed into the mess hall. It was already crowded with people arriving for the evening meal, but he disregarded them, and they him, and sat down where he had a good view of a multipanel.

The first pictures were blurred and indistinct, but it was only a minute before the circuits stabilized, and all of a sudden, there it was—their destination, so sharp he felt he could reach out and touch it.

It's—well, it's like coming home.

There, in real time, were things he had only ever seen before in still pictures: native plants waving in a gentle breeze, their broad, flat leaves bluer than those of Earth, white surf breaking on a long low line of rocks, clouds turning to crimson as the sunset reddened them.

A vast ache grew, centered on his heart, and he found he had to blink away tears.

Around him the Tripborn came and went, collecting their food, eating it, disposing of the utensils for recycling. But the Earthborn—they understood what these pictures signified! They let their meals grow cold, untasted, hardly daring to blink for fear they would miss something crucial, despite the fact that the signals were being recorded—and anyhow there would be more tomorrow and the next day.

He himself did not glance around when someone dropped into the next chair to his, though he recognized Tsien from the corner of his eye. He breathed, "Isn't it *wonderful?*"

"No," the psychologist said curtly. "It's terrible."

"What?" That did jolt him into turning around, and he saw the psychologist's face, eloquent of gloom. "I don't understand!"

"Don't you? Look at the Tripborn, then! Are they getting excited? The hell they are! Franz, we simply haven't reached them! Yet I've stepped up the 'leave-the-ship' commands to such a point that one of my own staff tried to walk out of an airlock an hour ago!"

"Earthborn?" Franz whispered.

"Earthborn? Yes, of course!" Tsien had brought a drink with him; he took a savage gulp from it. "What in the universe can we have done that the Earthborn are being affected and the Tripborn are ignoring our best efforts?"

Franz sat for a long moment in silence. Then, as though making confession of a deadly sin, he told Tsien about the picture of Mars he had believed he was projecting on the wall of his office.

"Yes, that fits," Tsien said dully. "Fits too well. Not that you should worry overmuch. Never before have humans born on Earth been subject to the strain we've undergone—your subconscious is simply sending reassuring messages to prop up your commitment. I agree about the example of Mars, and if we'd thought of the idea forty years ago, we'd have supplied Martian scenes just like that one for the library. But of course no one from Mars was included in the crew."

He took another swig of his drink. "If the phenomenon recurs," he said in something closer to his normal didactic tone, "ask Philippa for a sedative. In fact, I think I'd better authorize a general issue of tranquilizers to the Earthborn. What I shall have to do to kick the Tripborn off this ship is going to be very fierce. I'm warning you. And I dare not waste any more time on half-measures."

A final swallow drained his mug. He rose. "Yes," he said more to the air than to Franz. "Yes, we're going to have to pull out all the stops. Much as I hate the idea, there's no more choice."

From every multipanel in the ship the spy-eye transmission glowed. Restlessly wandering through his own section to check on the night shift, Franz visited the hydroponics room, the biolabs, the feedmix monitoring room, the master water-purification plant, the dietary and reclamation rooms—all those spaces that formed the lungs, heart, and digestive organs of the ship. The staff were engaged in their usual tasks, adjusting controls, testing the cultures, hunting diligently for the last traces of the sterile mutation that had caused so much anxiety.

He paused beside a young worker, not yet out of his teens, who was examining a sample of Culture B for the telltale darkening that betrayed the presence of infertile stock.

"What's the incidence of sterility now?" he said at random.

The boy turned calm eyes on him. "Down to half a per cent within the past hour. It's taken care of."

Irritated—by what, he could not tell—Franz said, "How are you going to like working with soil when we land?"

"I won't," said the boy, and poured his sample back into the semiliquid mass filling the culture tubes. Then he moved on to the next sampling outlet.

Franz did not try to stop him. There had been something terribly final about those two words. And not only final. Utterly honest.

But in which sense was he to take them? "I won't like it," or "I won't land"?

He thought again of what Tsien had said about pulling all the stops out and was shaken with a pang of mental agony.

We're having to force these people to complete the task we gladly gave up our lives for!

Somehow it seemed unworthy.

Yet there was no actual trouble. No overt resistance, no disobedience, even. Merely that continuing lack of exitement, that inhuman calmness, that absence of feeling that was more horrible than any violent reaction.

By the time they had entered orbit around Trip's End and it was announced that a landing boat was ready, Franz felt as though all the sadness of the universe had invaded and overcome his mind.

Nonetheless, it was with eagerness that he walked down corridors toward a section of the ship the existence of which he had almost forgotten. Ever since Sivachandra had let slip the identity of the young man who was to make the initial landing, he had meant to become acquainted with him; after all, he was going to be remembered by the colonists throughout their history. But days had slipped by, and there had been no time to do so. Now, as he scanned the group gathered at the boat lock, he had to think twice before he recognized Felipe: tall, black-haired, unsmiling, with deep-set dark eyes.

Sivachandra and Lola Kathodos were directing final tests of the boat's equipment; a group of orderlies from Medical, together with Tsien and some of his staff, surrounded the tall young pilot. As he approached, he caught Philippa's eye and wondered whether she, like himself, might be trying to recapture the emotion that had accompanied the making of this man.

It was pointless. They had, after the fashion that life in the ship permitted, been in love. But each, to the other, had inescapably been one of many, and now not even the dull embers of passion could be found in memory. All was ashes.

Instead of going up to Philippa, as he had half-intended, he turned aside to speak with Tsien, who looked cautiously optimistic.

"Is everything going all right?" he demanded.

"As far as we can tell. Medically he's in perfect shape, and last time he went through the simulator he coped with every emergency we could throw at him. He ought to have no difficulty at all. It's a very minor mission, this, you know—a matter of landing, taking some samples, and coming straight back."

Sivachandra called out, "Felipe, please get aboard now! We shall be launching you in mark plus seven minutes!"

Franz could stand back no longer. He pushed aside a couple of Tripborn medical orderlies and grasped Felipe's hand. "Good luck!" he said with fervency. "It's a great moment for us all!"

And then he turned slowly away. For there had been no reaction in the face of this son of his. There was no sense of history in him. He had been told to do a job, and he was about to do it, and that was all.

But we harped on the wonder of it, Franz raged silently within his mind. *We explained how marvelous it is that beings spawned in a chemical soup, mere smears of moisture on a ball of rock, should cross the gulf between the stars! And it is marvelous, it's amazing and fantastic—and they simply don't care!*

The door of the boat closed behind Felipe, and Tsien was touching Franz's arm.

"Let's go up to Navigation," he said softly. "The whole thing's being monitored from there."

VI

It seemed like an age before the telltales on the hull of the boat reported the first whispers of atmosphere. In the Navigation section a tense group of technicians faced the screens and instrument panels that kept contact with Felipe. At intervals he assured them in a flat voice that everything was working well.

Franz realized belatedly that Philippa was standing beside

him. In a gesture he was scarcely conscious of, so deep a need did it fulfill, he put his arm around her, and she flashed him a quick, wan smile.

The red surface of the planet loomed on the screens: Rough mountains gashed by narrow, swift-flowing rivers passed below the boat as it rushed toward the broad, flat plain beside the sea that had tentatively been selected for the settlement.

"I'm in sight of the target area," Felipe said at last. "Atmospheric conditions are satisfactory for a manual landing."

The reaction motors drowned out the next few words; down there, Franz knew, the boat must be slowing, then hovering, and now—yes, there was the faintest crunching noise!—making actual contact with the ground.

He made it!

The roaring that came over the microphones died away. But there was no further word from Felipe.

"Siv, is something wrong?" Magda rasped when the tension had become intolerable.

"Nothing!" Sivachandra answered, having checked every dial in sight. "Air's good—wind's negligible—the ground there is solid enough to bear the boat's weight. . . . Felipe!"

"Yes?" the pilot's voice came back after the inevitable brief delay due to distance.

"Are you proceeding with your postlanding drills?"

"N-no." The voice shook, this time, as though he was under impossible strain.

"Why not?"

"Because—"

And all of a sudden, Felipe screamed.

"Internal cabin viewer!" Sivachandra rapped, and the exterior picture shown on the screens was replaced by a view of the boat's cockpit—and of Felipe, screaming and screaming and tearing at his harness, his suit, his own skin. Blood ran under his nails.

"What's happened?" Magda shouted, and then interrupted herself. "Never mind! Remotes on! Get him back, *fast!*"

With silent speed the technicians obeyed. Before they had taken back control of the boat, however, Felipe had slumped in his seat, head lolling, mouth ajar, in a dead faint.

"Tsien!" Franz cried. "You didn't condition him right—you didn't prepare him for the shock of landing!"

"He could not have done so," said a quite voice. "We could have told you so. But we were sure you would not listen. You never listen to us, any more than you think for yourselves. Forty years ago or more you abdicated your powers of reason. That span of time is long enough."

The speaker was Quentin Hatcher, as Franz discovered in dismay when he turned to look down the length of the navigation room. He had moved to confront the Earthborn officers, and not only he, but every single Tripborn present, bar the technicians who were bringing back the boat.

"Since you have now seen for yourselves how futile your intended actions are," Hatcher went on, "you must resign yourselves to facts for a change. This is the end of your dream. We can no longer allow you to remain in control of this ship."

"Mutiny!" Magda shouted, her face twisted as though she had heard obscenities beyond description.

"Say rather that the real is supplanting the ideal," Hatcher countered. "We have no intention of harming you, of course. But we do insist on one thing. There must be no more talk of a landing on this planet."

"You're mad!" Hattus breathed huskily.

"Ask your psychologist whether he can confirm that accusation," Hatcher said. "I believe he is honest enough to tell the truth and contradict you. Have we not resisted, for fifteen days past, your best attempts to drive us out of our minds—and out of the ship?"

"You knew about the conditioning!" Tsien gasped.

"Why, of course. It was the work of a moment to pick Franz Yerring's pocket of his secret orders, read them through, and restore the envelope to its original state. When he put the drug into the food transformers, Tessa was right there, watching him."

"But you ate the food!" Franz broke in. "I know you did! I watched you! Where did you get the antidote?"

"There was no need for an antidote," Hatcher answered. "We knew that whatever you did would not affect us."

Franz felt Philippa collapse against him. Sivachandra had begun to sob, dry-eyed, and even the normally imperturbable Hattus was biting frenziedly at his nails. For all the Earthborn, this was indeed the death of a dream.

Yet there were harsh, intractable facts that meant that what Hatcher was demanding was out of the question. In a voice the steadiness of which surprised him, Franz heard himself say, "But we must land, Hatcher. Otherwise we shall starve and suffocate."

Hatcher shrugged. "We shall bring raw materials from the planet's surface. Since you Earthborn are so determined to set foot on this new world, we shall let you make the necessary journeys back and forth."

"But that won't work!" Franz insisted desperately. "Our boats are designed for shipping cargo down, not up! To bring up a ton of clean water would cost us forty tons of fuel—at best you could postpone the end by a couple of months."

"Then you must find an alternative solution," Hatcher said in an indifferent tone. "The fact stands: We Tripborn are not going to make another landing."

"I have the solution, then," Franz snapped. "Nominate one thousand people to be killed."

There was a shocked pause. For the first time ever, to Franz's knowledge, Hatcher's face betrayed a sign of emotion. In a completely changed voice he said, "What do you mean?"

"That's better. Start listening with your mind instead of your muscles! This ship is a closed ecological system. In theory it can be made indefinitely self-sufficient with no input other than radiation and interstellar gas. But it's overpopulated. You stand there and you tie up water, calcium, phosphorus, nitrogen, carbon, eighty or a hundred pounds of complex organic compounds in the form of brain, heart, liver, lungs, the rest. Now do you see what I'm getting at? We relied on opening the system when we reached Trip's End, to replenish the resources which are bound up in our bodies. So we have three choices."

He drew a deep breath. "Either we stay up here and die of hunger—or we stay up here and eat each other until the population drops—or we land. Which is it to be?"

I missed the fourth possibility, Franz thought dully. *We stay here and simply go insane.*

He paced restlessly up and down his office. There was nowhere else for him to go. All the Earthborn had been confined to quarters, efficiently, without fuss, but without mercy.

Three more days' reserves had been wasted. He could almost taste the foulness starting to taint the air, feel the ship dying like a man with a perforated intestinal ulcer.

Without warning the door opened, and he whirled to face it. Two stern-mannered Tripborn stood in the gap.

"Come with us," said the nearer, and he numbly obeyed.

They led him past Navigation, past Administration, until he knew what his destination had to be. Psychological. And there Tsien was sitting at his desk, sunken-cheeked, in company with George Hattus and Quentin Hatcher.

"So you're still fit to walk about, Franz," Hattus said with charnel humor, and Franz stiffened.

"What do you mean?"

"George and you and I," Tsien said, "are the only functioning Earthborn left in the ship. Everyone else has retreated into fugue—Magda, Siv, Lola, Phil, all of us."

"I . . ." Franz licked his lips, horrified. "But why?"

"Because," Tsien said, "Hatcher was quite right. We long ago abdicated our power of reason. We're faced with an intolerable decision. We have to plant the colony, and the Tripborn won't let us, and there's nothing we can do about the dilemma."

"Double bind," Hattus said with a shrug. "A classic route into insanity."

The words were plain enough, but they made no sense to Franz, and he said so. Tsien turned to Hattus.

"George, a demonstration, please."

From his pocket Hattus produced a folded sheet of paper. Before displaying it, he said, "Tell me, Franz, when you received your sealed orders, what was your reaction?"

"Well . . . Well, admiration, to be honest. At the genius which had prepared even for such a distant eventuality."

"Anything else?"

"A sense of fresh commitment, I suppose. New determination to see the project through. *Why?*"

"This is why," Hattus said, and displayed the sheet of paper. At its foot it bore a signature, unmistakably Yoseida's own.

Yes, the colony must succeed! But the Tripborn refuse to land. So we've failed. But we mustn't fail! We . . .

Suddenly the paradox was too much for him. He cried out and would have fallen but that Hatcher caught him, and he felt—just barely—the prick of a needle in his arm. But that was an intrusion. His mind was running round and round in a closed system: *land/can't land/must land/can't land . . .*

Slowly, however, the compulsive ideas cleared away, and he was able to focus his eyes on Tsien's anxious face.

"Better now?" the psychologist demanded.

"I . . . Yes, I'm okay. But what happened?" Franz freed himself from Hatcher's supporting hands and straightened unsteadily.

"Just now? You reacted in the way you were programmed to react more than forty years ago. You've always believed that you volunteered for this trip, haven't you?"

"But I did! Of course I did!"

Tsien shook his head. "No, you didn't. Any more than I did, or George, or any of us. We were conditioned with a posthypnotic compulsion, and one of the releasers is the sight of Yoseida's signature."

"I—I don't believe it!"

"You have to," Tsien said ruthlessly. "I've been stripping down my own mind, and George's, for the past forty-eight hours, ever since I realized how well the explanation fitted. And I've found the proof. Take my word for it, but I can back the claim up later if you like. What I've found shows that Yoseida, the idealist, the visionary dreamer, was a megalomaniac who could not be satisfied with less than a brand-new planet as a tribute to his memory."

"And stopped at nothing to make us obey the demands he put on us," said Hattus.

"But if it drove everyone else into fugue," Franz said foggily, "why did we escape the consequences of this compulsion?"

"You, I suspect," Tsien said, "because you had the most rational of all our reasons for requiring a landing. We have to break open the closed system of the ship or else we starve. George got away with it—I think—because his primary concern is and has always been with the smooth functioning of the ship, and there's no question but that the Tripborn do make it run smoothly. More so, indeed, than we Earthborn could ever hope to achieve. Even so, he's been in a bad state, shaking, his teeth chattering . . . And as for me, I suppose my training helped me to work out what had been done to my mind. Certainly it was what enabled me to believe that the conditioning could be counteracted."

Franz half-expected to find himself drowned in black despair; if he was to believe Tsien, he had to admit that he had sacrificed his life in vain. Yet somehow he remained calm enough to reason. Doubtless that was thanks to the drug he had just been given.

"But we still haven't solved anything," he said.

He turned to Hatcher. "Do we suffocate, or turn cannibal, or land?"

"We did not ask to be born to face this predicament," Hatcher said stonily. "You allowed it to be created. You must find the answer. Don't look to us."

"What—what do you intend to do?"

"Since you Earthborn are so set on planetary life, we shall land you. All of you. And leave you to survive as best you can. For us, the ship is all we know. We decline to leave."

Ship!

In a blinding instant of insight, Franz had the answer, and it was so dazzling that he almost fainted again.

"Tsien!" he barked. "Is it true that we Earthborn could be landed on the planet without reacting the way Felipe did?"

He did not have to ask what had happened to the poor devil; he had doubtless suffered the worst agoraphobia of any man ever born, the first time he found himself required to step out of a metal hull under a naked sky.

"Why . . ." Tsien licked his lips. "Why, I think so. If we can bring the rest of us back from catatonia, and I'm fairly certain that that can be managed."

"Then we shall land," Franz said simply.

"To found a colony ourselves?" Hattus demanded. "Franz, you still haven't solved the problem! There are only two hundred and fifty of us, and we were expecting to shed more like eighteen hundred of the crew before going back to—"

"No, not to found a colony! *To build another ship!*"

There was an instant of stunned silence. He rushed on. "Listten, listen! I've had nothing to do the past few days but figure and calculate, and I know it can be done. If we send only the Earthborn down to the planet, we can't last nearly long enough to tackle any major tasks—but if the Tripborn are willing to join us on a rota basis, say an extra two-fifty at a time, we can stabilize the ship's economy for at least five years. The Tripborn ought to be able to endure at least a short period on the planet, perhaps with the help of drugs and hypnosis, so long as they aren't threatened with the prospect of a permanent stay. Meantime the rest of them can assemble, with materials that we send up to orbit, another ship as large as this!"

"But it took ten years to build this one, with all the resources of Earth behind us!" Hattus snapped.

"We have the tools to build a town for ten thousand," Franz retorted. "What's more, the Tripborn, after working with the ship throughout their lives, must be able to do better than we could. They must have learned the lessons we didn't. Hatcher, could you not design an even better ship?"

They waited tensely for the Tripborn to consider his reply. When it came, it amounted to no more than a nod and a cocked eyebrow. But he spun on his heel and hastened from the room.

"I think he must have gone to consult the others," Franz said. "But I also think I've made my point."

"But what about us?" Tsien demanded. "We're conditioned, probably more deeply than I can remedy, to the idea of returning to Earth. We aren't equipped to establish the colony. Besides, though we may look young and fit enough, we're not in a physical state to breed another generation. We'd get amaurotic idiots, we'd get—"

"No, we don't found a colony!" Franz barked. "We go back to Earth just as we originally planned."

At the mention of that precious word, yearning showed in the faces of both his listeners, and he thought: *That's one thing they've lost, the Tripborn. The idea of going home. Because they are home. Already. Anywhere. Anywhere else.*

"But why does it have to end in this—this untidy way, this empty way?" Hattus pleaded. "With nothing to show for all our work?"

"On the contrary," Franz said. *Once there was a sea . . .* "We have everything to show for it.

"Think it through. The Tripborn didn't even worry about what Tsien did to try and drive them out of the ship, make them obey the command to land on the planet."

Tsien nodded. "And that's incredible. No human being should have been able to resist my methods. I told you: I pulled out all the stops."

"No human being," Franz said quietly. "There's your answer. The Tripborn aren't human any longer. They're—crew."

"But . . . !" Tsien's embryo objection died away, and after a second he gave a firm nod.

"Oh, yes. Oh, *yes!* That would account for everything: the smooth way they took the ship over from us, their calm efficiency, their—everything about them."

"But you can't go from human to nonhuman in one generation!" Hattus cried.

"Who's to say what the next after man can and cannot do?" Franz countered. "Man's done some extraordinary things, and leaving his own Solar System isn't the least amazing." He hesitated.

"You know, the idea only struck me just now, but the more I think about it, the more—the more *real* it seems. Long ago on Earth the sea was the only habitat of life, as it remains today, in all important respects, on that planet down there. But the seas grew crowded, and sometimes the tide stranded certain species in the shallows, and sometimes the shallows dried up. So a handful of creatures learned to take the sea ashore with them, just as we brought the air of Earth in this ship. The blood in your body now is precisely as salty as was that long-ago ocean. Of course, for a long while the animals had to come back to the water to breed.

"But—one day—one of them left the water and never came back.

"This isn't the end of mankind; there are still snakes and birds and dogs on Earth, still amphibians, even, which have to return to a pond and lay their eggs. That's what I think the Tripborn have become: amphibians, who will have to return to their rock pools, their planetary bases, when they want to reproduce. But that need only be a temporary phase. The ship we are going to build here will teach the Tripborn how to breed. And after the amphibian, there will be a snake, and a bird, and a dog—"

The certainty was growing; he could *feel* it.

"And in the end," Franz said slowly, "there will be a man."

NO OTHER GODS BUT ME

I

For Colin Hooper, looking back on it later, the first part of the adventure had the quality of a dream. He could hardly convince himself it had really happened—or, granting it had, that it had happened to him and not to someone else.

Eventually it turned from dream to nightmare, but in the instant of the lightning strike, to which he afterward dated the start of it all, he had no thought for anything except the way in which London's disgusting summer weather was ruining his attempts to escape from black depression.

The lightning showed him Tippet Lane, one of the tiny streets—alleys, rather—in the vicinity of Shepherd Market. It was only some four paces wide. Fed up with huddling in the shelter of an awning, he decided to take the risk and cross over.

As though some celestial scrubwoman had chosen the same moment to empty her colossal bucket over the city, the downpour redoubled.

Gasping, feeling it might be physically possible to drown in a storm so thick, he scrambled into the embrasure of a doorway. The last layer of his clothing was saturated now; his feet squelched horribly in his shoes, and everything clung clammily to his skin.

"Christ, what a night!" he exploded, noticing only after he had spoken that the doorway was already occupied—by a woman. He caught the gleam of street lamps on the wet fabric of her hooded raincoat as she turned and glanced at him. His automatic guess was that she must be one of the streetwalkers who haunt the Shepherd Market area.

Maybe she could lift him out of his sullen rage against the world . . . ? No. The hell. The mood had eaten too deeply into his soul. He'd never gone for the commercial bit, anyhow. Besides, her response to his exclamation didn't fit the role he'd guessed at for her.

"Yes, bloody, isn't it? If we don't get some real summer some time, I think I'll go out of my mind."

Which was not unfriendly, perhaps an invitation to pass the time in conversation until the rain let up. But he wasn't in the right frame of mind for idle chat. With water trickling out of his hair, he stared morosely at the street.

The rain pounded and bounced on the ground. Cold wind picked up the droplets as they shattered and tossed them mistlike between the buildings. An occasional halfhearted tremor of thunder shivered in the distance.

July in London couldn't always be like this, surely! Nobody could live in such a country! No, this must be as exceptional as the English claimed. The girl had said, just now, she was hoping for some "real summer," and she sounded like a Londoner—as far as his American ear could tell, she'd spoken with an outright cockney accent, her *o* sounds shading into *ow*. . . .

It wouldn't make much difference in his present drenched state whether he stayed in shelter or walked out into the road; still, it was marginally warmer away from the wind. Resigning himself to a long wait, he fished in his pocket for a pack of cigarettes and wordlessly offered one to his chance companion. She accepted with a murmur of thanks. When he selected one for himself, his wet fingertips left dark marks on the pale paper.

As she bent, a moment later, to use his lighter, he saw her face clearly for the first time and had such a shock he let the flame go out.

"Why—it's you!"

"What on earth do you mean?" the girl said, jerking back her head.

Colin's mind raced, replaying in memory the single phrase she'd uttered as he joined her in the doorway. Of course: not cockney, but Australian. He'd simply not expected to hear an Aussie voice in the middle of London—though why not, since the city was constantly flooded with visitors from all parts of the Commonwealth, he couldn't have said.

"You're from Melbourne," he said positively.

"Why . . ." She was staring unashamedly at him. "Yes, I am! But you're never from down under. You're an American, aren't you?"

"Yes."

There was a moment of bewildered silence broken only by distant traffic noise and the splashing of the rain. Then she said firmly, "Light!"

"What? Oh—sorry." From the far reach of his astonishment he came back to the present and flicked his forgotten lighter again. But it wasn't for her cigarette that she required it. Taking his wrist in capable fingers, she lifted the flame so that its thin yellow glow could play on his face and show her its slightly sallow complexion—testifying to the absence of a summer in this year of his life—the dark red, water-slicked hair, the brown eyes, the mouth that seemed to have lost the trick of smiling.

"Okay, I don't know you," she said finally, and drew the lighter to her cigarette. "So how the blazes could you be so sure I hail from Melbourne?"

"I noticed you there," Colin said, and having lit his own cigarette put out the lighter. Lacking it, he could not see anything in the shadow of her raincoat hood, but he was absolutely certain of what he would have seen had there been light: the quizzical expression in her violet eyes, the slight tilt at the corners of her overlarge mouth, perhaps a faint wrinkling of her wide white forehead under raven hair.

"When?"

"About three months ago. The first time standing at a bus stop. The second time in the bar of the Crux Hotel. And the third time having dinner in the Cresco Restaurant."

"I've been in those places," she agreed. "I—uh—I have to be honest, though. I don't remember noticing you."

Colin thought bitterly: *It would be best for me to lie and not admit why I remember you so clearly. . . .*

A surge of recollection, chillier even than the wind, blotted out his mind momentarily, and he was on the point of deciding that he could not bear to pursue the conversation when there was a noise at his side.

The door against which they stood huddled had swung ajar with a faint swishing and was now fully open, revealing the interior of the building. But no details could be made out, only a sort of misty blue light that seemed to be shed from the very air.

The girl gave a gasp and moved automatically closer to him, putting her hand on his arm. He was out of the habit of being touched; he found the contact irritating and would have shaken loose had not a deep voice addressed them from somewhere out of sight.

"Come in, please, and welcome! The rain will not stop for a long while yet, and it cannot be pleasant to stand out of doors in damp clothing."

Literally to run into a girl whom he'd last seen the other side of the Earth was a surprise big enough to last Colin for more than one evening, but at least there could be a conventional explanation for the meeting. Coincidences, after all, do happen. To be invited to enter a totally strange building, by someone who was nowhere in view, was something else again.

The girl seemed eager enough to comply. "Anywhere is better than Tippet Lane in a cloudburst," she muttered. "And doesn't it feel lovely and warm in there?"

"Do come in," the voice urged. "We realize this is unexpected, but there's no cause to be afraid!"

"I don't like this," Colin said abruptly. "Who'd think of asking us not to be afraid if there *was* nothing to worry about?"

The argument told, but only for a few seconds. "Stay out and freeze if you like," the girl snapped, and stepped over the threshold.

Reluctant, he accompanied her. The first pace he took informed him why there had been a swishing noise as the door opened; it had brushed the immensely deep pile of a fabulously luxurious carpet. But that was all he learned immediately. Even compared to the gloom outside, the bluish light in here was very dim, and it took his eyes long moments to adjust.

When they did, he was inclined to disbelieve what they reported. The place where he found himself seemed impossibly large, as though it extended a mile to left and right. A clever illusion, doubtless—but he wished he knew how it had been accomplished.

And why.

Ahead of them the deep carpet stretched toward a flight of low steps, with four or five risers reaching a height of perhaps two feet. Seeming to float above a dais that formed a continuation of the topmost tread, a disc of whitely luminous material blended into the blue-mist twilight, like a low sun on a foggy day.

"I—I wasn't expecting this at all," the girl said in a thin voice.

So what were you expecting? Entrée to some Mayfair playboy's swank apartment?

But Colin had no chance to utter the sour comment nor to do as he most wanted, take her arm and turn her by force back to the door. For the speaker who had invited them in chose now to reveal himself.

Almost invisible in a pool of shadow beside the glowing white disc, still as a statue in a robe that flowed silk-even to his feet, he surveyed them with his face a mask of darkness, for the light did not reach above his shoulders.

"You," he said at length, "are Vanessa Sheriff?" It was as though the words emanated from the air rather than from a human mouth; none could be seen in that shadow-blank visage.

The girl gave a little shiver. "How did you—?"

The man ignored her. "And you are Colin Hooper?"

"What the hell business is it of yours?" Colin rasped, his mind suddenly full of indescribable terror at hearing his name spoken by this improbable and anonymous stranger.

"Look!" the man commanded, a sudden ring of authority in his booming tone. He flung up his arm and stabbed a long finger toward the white disc. In spite of his determination to turn and run, Colin found he had been deceived into obedience; found, too, that that disc was no flat plate of featureless luminance, as he had formerly assumed. There was motion on its surface, spiral motion, as though from its edges a river of light were pouring into a whirlpool at its center. Fascinated against his will, he tried to follow the streaming pattern, tracing time after time from edge to center, edge to center, edge to center . . .

II

His arms and legs were stiff, and he was very cold. He fumbled for lost blankets, thinking himself in bed, until the question of how a mattress could be this hard penetrated his dull mind. Blinking open his eyes, he looked up into darkness.

There was a sound of moaning from nearby, a girl's voice, and everything came back with a rush.

He sat up. He was on the floor of a dusty room, vacant except for boxes stacked in piles against the wall. A thin wash of yellow light flooded through a narrow window and played over the ceiling. A street lamp, he reasoned foggily. By its aid he crossed the floor on hands and knees to where the girl lay and gently shook her awake.

Vanessa—he scarcely recalled how he knew her name—rose shakily to her feet, leaning on him for support. She took in their surroundings with effortful slowness, as though postponing the moment when she must confront the impossible.

"Are you all right?" Colin asked inanely.

"I—I think so." She rubbed her hand, grimy with the dirt of the floor, across her forehead, leaving a broad smeared mark. Breaking free of his support, she walked unsteadily across the room, pausing twice: once by the door next to the window, once by another door set in the opposite wall. She did not try to open either, but returned to his side.

"What is this place?" she demanded, accepting Colin's offer of a cigarette, crumpled because he had lain on the pack, but intact.

"I've no idea. I haven't had time to look it over." He put away his lighter and produced a pen-size flashlight, which he shone rapidly around.

"Well, a real boy scout!" Vanessa said with feeble mockery. "Prepared for everything, aren't you?"

"I'm not in a joking mood," he retorted.

"Nor am I. Sorry. I just feel that if I don't laugh I shall scream. . . ." The admission trailed away. "There's something written on those cartons. Can you read it?"

Colin aimed the little yellow beam and read aloud: "Jean Duval Friction Tonic, for salon use only. We must be in the storeroom of a barber shop."

"Great," she said. "Just great. So what?"

He did not reply, but continued his survey. Other cartons

contained shampoo, shaving sticks, razor blades, all mundane enough. He checked the door leading into the building, but it proved to be securely locked.

He glanced at his watch, having to tilt his arm at an awkward angle to catch the light from the window. "Funny!" he said after a brief hesitation. "It says about ten of nine. But it was nearly that when I—uh—bumped into you. And I have a feeling that hours must have passed."

"So do I," Vanessa agreed. "Or maybe years."

"Don't you have a watch?"

"Yes." She displayed it. "A very good one. It was a present only a week or two ago. It's electric—you know, one of the kind that run a year on a tiny little battery? But it seems to have stopped at quarter to nine. Has yours stopped?"

Rather foolishly, he set his wrist to his ear. "No, it's ticking clear as a bell," he announced. And then added abruptly, "Let's get the hell out of here!"

"If we can," Vanessa sighed.

Producing his flashlight again, Colin turned to the street door. He discovered a bolt, which he drew back with an oilless screech, a security chain, which he let fall with a rattle, and a Yale lock, which he turned without trouble.

"I'll be damned," he said. "We're still in Tippet Lane."

No doubt of it. The same street, the same doorway, even the same rain, although now it had thinned to the type of drizzle the English impolitely term a "Scotch mist." With Vanessa at his heels, he stepped over the threshold and stared about him in bewilderment—then snatched at her hand and drew her close, slamming the door.

"Policeman!" he whispered.

She understood at once and put her arm around him as though they were doing no more than taking shelter. To have to explain at this time of night—and much time must have elapsed, for the city-wide drone of traffic had faded to almost nothing—what they were doing in the storeroom of a shop was more than he could cope with.

The rain-caped figure of the patroling constable drew level; from beneath the dark conical helmet unfriendly eyes studied them.

"Don't you two have homes to go to?" the man said after a long, meaning pause.

"Ah . . . Ah, sure we do," Colin said. His mind was racing, but he knew how unconvincing—how guilty—he must sound. Vanessa leapt into the breach.

"Is it very late, Officer? We've sort of lost track of the time, if you see what I mean."

"Yes, ma'am. It's very late. It's ten past three," the constable said. "And it's no night to stand around snogging. Particularly not in doorways like that one."

He waited for them to move off, embarrassed as children caught stealing cookies, and when Colin glanced back he saw, as he had expected, that the constable was testing the door to make sure it was locked.

"Lucky it was a Yale," Vanessa said caustically. Now she was in the fresh air again, she seemed to have recovered her self-possession. "Come on, this way."

Glad to be taken in charge, Colin followed her dumbly, and in a couple of hundred yards they reached Piccadilly, empty of traffic bar a cruising cab dutifully halted at a red light. Then he finally connected with what the policeman had said.

"Ten after three!" he burst out, and a second later let go a resounding sneeze. Small wonder, if he had spent six hours in these soaking clothes stretched out on a bare floor.

Or—had he?

"I'd like to take another look at that place," he said suddenly.

"So would I," Vanessa agreed. "But with that nosy copper hanging around . . . What do you make of it?"

"Nothing," he grunted. "All I know is, we've lost about six hours, and—" The words were cut short by another sneeze. At once she became solicitous and felt his sleeve.

"Why, you're wringing wet! I should have thought. You don't even have a raincoat on! Here, you'd better come up to my place and get dried off. It's only a few minutes' walk."

"So's my hotel," Colin said. "I don't have to put you to the trouble."

"Trouble be damned," she said, and shivered visibly. "Look, do you think I could shake hands and march off as though nothing's happened? What we've been through is the weirdest experience of my life, and I have this feeling that if I let you out of my sight, I'll never find you again and so I'll never make myself believe the truth in the morning. I'll more likely wind up thinking I'm out of my mind!"

"That's exactly how I feel," Colin admitted after a second's hesitation.

"Then don't argue. Come along."

Briskly she turned back the way they had come. They walked for only the brief time she had promised, but so confusing was the maze of streets that Colin became hopelessly lost at once.

Silence fell between them. It lasted until they had climbed steep, narrow stairs and entered a small but well-furnished three-room apartment with modern décor and some good modern paintings on the walls. It lasted beyond that, even though Colin wanted to break it, while she turned on the heat and vanished into some other room.

He was thinking of another home he'd been invited into, that also belonged to a girl with raven hair, and wondering for the ten thousandth time how it hadn't led him to a happy marriage.

She's not really like Esther at all, and yet in so many ways I'm reminded, I'm reminded: not the face but the expression, not the figure but the way she walks....

But the shock of the breakup had shattered his mind to such a depth he sometimes wondered whether he would recognize Esther if he encountered her on the street. He had been left with the feeling that he had never learned to know her at all, that they had remained strangers even at the tumultuous height of their affair.

"Bathroom's through there—take a hot shower if you like."

He came back to the present with a jolt; she was offering him a towel and a terry-cloth robe.

"And there's an airing cupboard. Put your clothes in there."

Turning away, she caught sight of herself in a mirror and grimaced at the smeared dirt on her forehead. "You should have told me about that," she muttered. "But never mind. I can wash in the kitchen. Want some coffee?"

Ten minutes, and he felt human again, thanks to the healing heat of the shower. Drying off, he donned the robe. It was intended for someone taller and leaner than his stocky five foot eight, but it was admirably cozy. Barefoot, he emerged into the living room again and found Vanessa pouring the promised coffee into two huge mugs, dark hair combed to new sleekness, ivory skin washed free of makeup and glowing by contrast to the dark-red housecoat she had changed into.

"Milk and sugar?" she said, not glancing up.

Good to have a commonplace question to answer....

"Black with two."

She handed him his mug and gave him a thoughtful up-and-down glance. "The gown isn't your size, I'm afraid. Still, it's better than wet clothes. Sit down."

He sank on to a long couch, his body going limp with relief.

He had not realized until this moment how terrified he had been by his extraordinary experience and still was unwilling to think about it. At random he said, "You have a nice place here."

"Thanks. But it isn't mine. It's my boy friend's, same as that gown you're wearing. He's in films."

He gazed at her blankly; she chuckled.

"Oh, don't worry! He's shooting on location. I think in Northumberland, he said. He loaned me the apartment while he's away. But for which I'd probably be on the streets, just as that damned copper seemed to think I was. . . ." She sipped her coffee, found it too hot to drink, and leaned back against the arm of a chair facing him, long, bare, lovely legs outstretched.

"Colin!"

Hearing her use his name for the first time gave him a ridiculous fluttering of the heart, as though he were a susceptible teenager. He was startled but delighted; he had been afraid he might never register such an emotion again after the way his separation from Esther had burned him out.

"Yes, Vanessa!"

"Is there any point in discussing what happened?"

He pondered for a long time. At last he shook his head.

"I'd like to. But it felt more like—well, a vision than a real event!"

She nodded, staring at the carpet. "I know what you mean. It didn't connect with real life. And I don't mean in the way that sometimes happens, when you shake your head and shake your head over some unaccountable little episode, and then years later someone gives you the missing bit of the puzzle—like tells you about the mess someone was in—and you say Christ, of course, *that* must have been why! But I've got to talk about it, even if we don't make any sense of it! Could it have been some crazy new society gimmick? Some weird party that'll show up in tomorrow's gossip columns?"

"What kind of party?"

She made a vague gesture. "Oh, one that involves luring strangers off the street and dumping them in some fantastic happening-type environment, then laughing at them from behind a screen. . . ." Her voice faded, and she glanced up. "No, not very convincing, is it?"

"Not if it leads to them being doped and left to wake up in the back of a barber shop."

She nodded. "And yet—and yet I must have something to hook on to! Colin, it's too much of a coincidence that you should have noticed me in Melbourne, then turned up in Tippet Lane at the very moment when . . ." She hesitated. "But how could it have anything to do with meeting you?"

"I've no idea," Colin said, and felt a shiver run down his spine.

"Well—well, talk to me, anyhow. To begin with: What the hell were you doing in Australia?"

III

Dare I be honest . . . ?

He was still too shaken to reach a decision. In a voice that astonished him with its calmness, he said, "No, I don't want you drawing ridiculous conclusions."

"What do you mean?"

"Well, if it was meeting me which—which triggered off what happened, it must have been me who brought you to London. Logical?"

She almost laughed. "Oh, you'd have to be a sinister mastermind to manage that! How I got here was perfectly ordinary. I fell for a confidence trick! And yet . . ." She paused.

"No, perhaps it was extraordinary. It was certainly very *peculiar*. You see, I'm an actress. Resting, in the cant phrase. I wish I'd stayed home, I really do, but . . . Well, I don't mean to imply that I'm no good, because I am, and I have a good fat cuttings book stuffed with rave reviews to prove the fact. I was in two movies that made money and another that should have done but didn't, and I felt I was ready for the—the big time. Australia is a trifle larger than a pocket handkerchief, you know, but success down under isn't what you'd call *success*, if you get me.

"So when I was offered a contract to make a film here in London, I jumped at it. Sold up my home, kissed my boy friends good-by, and climbed aboard the next plane.

"And . . . Oh, it was completely crazy. My agent back home, who's as case-hardened as they come, said the deal was solid. I still have the actual contract, or at any rate a photostat. And what do I find when I get here? Nothing! The guy who hired me has never been heard of. There's no company registered in the name of the documents. It's all blown away like—like morning mist! The only possible explanation is that I got caught up in a confidence trick, as I said. But it can't have been aimed at me because I don't have any money; all I had was my home, my belongings, and enough to pay my one-way air fare." She spread her hands helplessly.

"So if it hadn't been for Larry, I don't know what I'd have done."

"Larry?"

"Larry Adderley. This is his place. I met him in a pub in Wardour Street. And we got talking, and . . . Well, he bailed me out. Otherwise I'd have collapsed with the screaming meemies. Just as I felt like doing tonight in Tippet Lane."

She raised her dark, keen eyes to his face. "Okay, now you know what brought me to England. I still want to know what brought you to Australia *and* England."

Colin hesitated but finally forced himself to a decision. If he didn't talk about his troubles to anyone, ever, he would wind up with them enclosed and rotten in his mind, souring everything else he did. And it might be easier to broach the truth to a complete stranger first of all.

He said, "Okay. I'm recovering from a nervous breakdown. Only that's a—what did you call it?—a 'cant phrase.' What it means is that I was off my head for a while, and I'm extremely used to things breaking into my life which aren't really there. I had actual and literal hallucinations."

She stared at him for the space of a dozen heartbeats. At last she said, reaching for a box of cigarettes on a nearby table, "No wonder you were so shaken by what happened tonight. If it's any consolation, we shared it, so that rules out hallucination in this case. But what—uh—caused the breakdown?"

He contrived a hollow laugh. "A good old-fashioned melodramatic reason. A broken heart." He couldn't keep his eyes on her; the more he looked at her, the more he saw how she was different from Esther, and the more he realized she was different, the more intolerable became the idea of talking about his lost love.

Instead, letting words come of their own accord, he scanned the books ranked in a case to her right, past her shoulder: a curious mixture, about one-third plays, one-third detective novels, and one-third works on philosophy and the occult. The boy friend—what was he called? Larry!—must have highly individual tastes.

"In some ways," he said, "our affair was a dry run for the aftermath. I mean, we were crazy about each other. Drunk. Addicted. So when we broke up, it was like taking a cold-turkey cure."

"What did break you up?"

"That's the hell of it." Colin clenched his fists. "I don't know! I don't believe she does, either. It simply flew to pieces —stopped—went bad. Overnight. Oh, I can't tell you any more than that!" He was digging his nails so hard into his palms he thought they might bleed.

"Sometimes," Vanessa said at length, "I envy people who can feel deeply. Me, I'm a main-chance type. Here I am living on Larry's back, and I don't give a hoot for the things he cares about. I simply don't have any contact with them. He's on a mystical kick, for example." She picked up a magazine from the table beside the cigarette box and displayed the title: *Dawn of Truth*. "Not that it makes any odds. Far as I'm concerned, he's a nice guy who was kind to me when I landed in a hell of a mess, and that's enough. . . . But what brought you to Melbourne and then London? Taking a round-the-world rest cure, hm?"

Colin managed a smile at that. "In a way, yes. I work for the personnel selection department of a chemical corporation, and I must say I couldn't have been treated better. First off, they cooled down my delusions with a new drug they haven't marketed yet—though I guess that wasn't entirely disinterested on their part. . . . But I'm grateful, anyway. I was in a world of cruel black shadows, and I couldn't break loose. Then when I was well enough, they said instead of going straight back to the office would I join a recruiting team they were sending out on a world tour. We lost some of our very top research people at the end of last year, and they were determined to pick up the best available replacements. And in fact, we've filled the vacancies now; this visit to London is more of a vacation than anything because we knew even before we left Australia that we were going to hire just one man, and we got him. So I wound up with four or five days to spare, to amuse myself. Only"—his mouth twisted—"I seem to have forgotten how."

"They must think very highly of you," Vanessa said, giving him another of her searching head-to-toe glances.

"I guess so. And—and paradoxically I resent it. Because in sheer fairness I have to go back to my desk next week and work like hell to repay them for their kindness, and what I really want to do is go mope in a shack in Mexico."

There was more silence after that. During it, her eyes drifted shut, and it dawned on him that she must be worn out. Yet it seemed like too great an effort to rise, find his clothes again, take his leave. . . . The rain had once more grown heavy; it drummed hypnotically at the windows like the fingers of an idiot.

"Colin," she said at last, eyes still closed. "That whirling disc. Don't hypnotists use something of the sort?"

He slapped his thigh. "I knew it reminded me of something! Yes, I've read about that, though I never saw one. But can we have been hypnotized? I thought the subject had to cooperate before that became possible."

"And I certainly wasn't cooperating," she said. "I'd just decided you were right to warn me not to do as I was told, you know. I felt I'd walked clean out of the ordinary world. Maybe on to one of these 'planes' that Larry's friends talk about. Have you ever taken acid? I was wondering if there could have been something in the air."

It was an idea that had not occurred to Colin. He was still debating with himself when there came a loud bang at the door.

She jolted upright, eyes snapping open. "Now for heaven's sake who can that be? Oh, some busybody from downstairs, I suppose! Larry warned me these floors and walls are like cardboard, for all the rent they charge! You stay put, and I'll sort the bugger out."

She strode to the door and flung it open.

But the man outside did not look at all like a sleepless neighbor. He wore a long dark overcoat, and he bore himself with conscious dignity. His hair, brown and crisp, was oddly cut, as though meant to be concealed under a headdress that was not a hat. Though his clothes fitted him excellently, he seemed self-conscious in them. Colin was reminded of someone who has been persuaded to attend a costume ball against his will.

"Are you Vanessa Sheriff?" the stranger demanded in a resonant voice.

Bewildered, Vanessa could only nod.

"And is your companion Colin Hooper?"

A hint of shrillness rode her reply, like the bright line down the blade of a new-honed knife. "What the hell does that have to do with you? I'm sick of people asking whether I'm me! *Get lost!*"

Colin had come to stand at her shoulder, the overlong robe flapping at his ankles. The stranger stared at him.

"Yes, you are Hooper," he said. "Well, then, all I can do is speak a warning. You will not understand, but I must beg you, beseech you, to take me seriously." He clasped his hands in supplication.

"Listen! You must both go away! Very far away from here, and separately! Each must go alone, or you will be in dreadful danger!"

"Who the hell are you?" Colin rasped, and Vanessa uttered a high, near-hysterical laugh.

"What does it matter? He's obviously nuts!"

"My name," the man said, "is Kolok. Not that that will signify anything to you." He preserved his dignity unruffled, although the tone of pleading did not leave his voice. "You know nothing about me. I assure you, though, I know much about you, including things you yourselves are unaware of. Sir, if you care at all for this young woman, you will do as I request. Go! Go very far away, and at once!"

Colin put his arm around Vanessa, who was trembling so much she could not speak.

"If there is one thing I won't do," he said in a clear hard tone, "it's what you just ordered me to do. Vanessa and I had never spoken to each other before tonight. As far as I know, we may never meet again. But if there is anything in the world which might make me want to do so, it's having a complete stranger barge in in the middle of the night and tell me to clear off!"

"Then I have failed," Kolok said. "They have been too clever for me." His shoulders hunched as if under a load of apprehension too great for any man to bear, and a gust of wet wind rattled the windows like a drum roll. After an eternal moment he turned away.

"Wait!" Colin exclaimed. He shot out his hand to touch the shoulder of Kolok's long dark coat. The cloth was dry; the shine on his shoes, or maybe boots, was undulled.

"You're dry!" he said unbelievingly. "But it's raining! It's been raining all night!"

"Not on the road by which I came," said Kolok.

A last flicker of hope, a final mute appeal, sparked in his eyes, but before Colin could react to that extraordinary statement, Vanessa had drawn him firmly back into the room and slammed the door.

Shaking, she leaned against it and thrust aside a lock of hair that had strayed over her forehead. She said, not looking at him, "Damn it, Colin, you're my type. Bloody-minded."

"What?" He blinked at her.

"You said to him exactly what I wanted to say, only I couldn't find the words. I was thinking yes, I'll pull myself together enough to calm down, say good night to this friendly stranger, write off what happened as just one of those things you have to live with . . . But having him show up! No! That's too much! Talking as though meeting you is important, in some fantastic way I shan't ever understand! Telling you to go away, fast, on his bare word! I can't make sense of it, and I don't ever hope to, but—oh, Christ, Colin, you mustn't leave me alone!"

Her hand groped along the wall and found the light switch. In sudden darkness she came to him, and her face was wet with tears.

For him, it was a healing and also the moment at which the events that had preceded it began to feel like a dream—a good dream, which went from terror and tears to contentment and relaxation, and no farther. For the time being, at any rate.

What it was for her he did not ask for fear of spoiling it for both of them.

Sufficient that it was what it was and that they both imagined it to be a completion. She was not yet awake when he stole away, but there was a smile on her face.

But the dream was not over after all. When it resumed, it was in New York, and there it turned to walking, waking nightmare.

IV

For Colin that encounter held the promise of salvation. He had been reminded that sharing was still possible, even though the one he shared with was not Esther. In gray morning light he made the deliberate decision to limit the experience: He kept his eyes on the sidewalk as he regained his hotel for fear he might read a street name and be able to find his way back. Later he rejected the idea of revisiting Tippet Lane in search of something more than the prosaic reality of dusty cartons to which he had awakened.

What he wanted was to believe that he had imagined something absolutely good, the total inverse of the hideous hauntings that had plagued him during his time of suffering.

A month passed, six weeks, and he was half-convinced that all had indeed been illusion, that his subconscious had sent him a signal to advise him that he was on the way to being whole.

He had been speaking literally when he told Vanessa that he was used to unreality in his life. He knew it was futile to question the foul black shapes he had confronted; it was a comfort to think that there had also been an unreality that was utterly delightful.

And then, on the Sunday before Labor Day . . .

He was not quite ready to look around for a woman who might take Esther's place—if any woman ever could—but he was contented enough to be back home after his trip around the world, after brief exposure to so many towns and cities like shots montaged in a movie. Life, on the whole, was being kind to him again.

So it suited his mood to spend the holiday by himself in the city. On the Sunday he went, as he often did during the summer, to listen to the folksingers gathered in Washington Square. The day was hot and close, and somehow the proceedings never took fire. Reluctant to admit that their expectations were not to be fulfilled, non-Villagers—tourists, even though they might hail from no farther away than the mid-Eighties—hung on and hung on: five o'clock, half past . . . while, perched on the rim of the dry pool around the fountain, a few singers argued desultorily about what number they should tackle next.

As disappointed as any out-of-town visitor and equally determined to stretch the time spent in the square in the hope of some last-minute excitement, Colin drifted from group to group discovering a minimum of talent and a maximum of frustration.

Finally, having overheard a knowledgeable young man explain to a friend that everybody who was anybody had gone to perform at a big festival in Pennsylvania, he gave up and decided to find a beer. Turning to work his way out of the small crowd of thirty or forty people he was immersed in, he saw Vanessa.

At first he literally refused to believe his eyes. He told himself he had been deceived by a chance resemblance, as he had been when he first spotted her in Melbourne, and then he frantically cast around for reasons to believe that it was *not* Vanessa because she belonged to an unreal world.

Wasn't that dark hair too short?

Yes, but she could have had it cut, and it was drawn back from *her* face.

Those violet eyes: covered by dark glasses, so he could not see their color!

Yet the glasses had turned to him and fixed him, so he had to stand stock-still.

She wore a yellow shirt, tight black pants, open sandals, no jewelery except . . .

On the ring finger of her left hand, a plain gold band.

And then it was too late. She was within arm's reach, smiling, saying, "Colin, how wonderful to see you!"

"What the hell are you doing in New York?" he demanded.

"Well! That's not the friendliest greeting I ever had!" But she laughed. "Oh, I came over with Larry. Kind of a working honeymoon!"

"You got married?"

"Yes. Don't you want to kiss the bride?" And she offered her cheek in mocking pantomime. Having no alternative, he brushed it with his lips, then glanced around.

"Is he here? Larry, I mean?"

"Oh, he's tied up with business of his own. One of these mystical things—I told you, I don't take much interest in that side of his life." She removed the dark glasses, and her eyes were dancing. "Colin, it's marvelous to run into you like this! Are you in a hurry?"

He had to shake his head from mere honesty.

"Then let's go find somewhere where the air conditioning is turned to 'very cold.' This muggy heat is making me wilt like an old flower."

She took his arm as though they had been friends for years, and perforce he had to walk along.

They strolled down Macdougal Street to the Firenze and sat by the window on hard wrought-iron chairs, their bare forearms cooling on the stone top of the table that divided them. At first their conversation consisted mainly of smiles, as though each was afraid of making direct reference to their meeting in London for fear of reviving a quiescent terror. Finally Colin took the plunge.

"Didn't you say your husband is an actor? You told me he was shooting in the country when I met you."

"Not an actor, a director."

"And is he making a picture here?"

"No . . ." She hesitated. "No, what he's doing, he's organizing a big international rally. Sort of a ceremony, in fact. For this mystical cult he belongs to, as I said. Me, I'm just along for the ride. We didn't have a honeymoon, and this—well, this is what I'm getting."

She chuckled, but the sound was hollow. Colin said, "I remember you mentioned his friends who talk about 'astral planes.' Is it a spiritualist group?"

She shook her head. The subject, clearly, made her sad; it showed in the sudden downturn of her mouth and the way she avoided his eyes, focusing instead on a picture behind him.

"Colin!" she said abruptly, and checked, as though changing her mind about what she had intended to say.

"Yes?"

"Oh, damn! I have no right to talk about my troubles to you. Really you're a total stranger."

"No, we aren't strangers."

"But we are! What do we have in common? Something weird that happened to us both, which—I'll bet—you've been living down ever since, just as determinedly as I have. Aren't I right?"

Colin hesitated, then at last gave a nod.

"I thought so. I remember you said you were used to unreal things breaking into the world, so perhaps it wasn't as tough for you as it was for me. But so far as I was concerned, it was—well—*awful*. Losing six hours, having that incredible stranger show up . . ." She drew a deep breath, and her lovely face grew hard with unhappiness.

"I think it must have been because of that, that I've behaved like a damned fool for the latest of many times in my life."

"Go on," Colin said neutrally. He was as yet uncertain whether he cared enough even to sympathize; he was too relieved to have found a way back to a stable existence for himself.

Twisting the gold ring on her left hand, she said, "I—I told you, didn't I, how I envy people who can feel deeply? Me, I'm a shallow person. I don't get stirred up by my emotions; I always seem to stand back and analyze them, even when they're happening. Perhaps that's what turned me into a competent actress: being able to recreate the image in the head. . . . But images are no bloody good when it comes to falling in love, which is something I don't think I've ever managed, though I've told myself so. And Larry was so kind to me, and in many ways he's the same kind of person I am—doesn't get angry easily, doesn't talk all the time about his likes and dislikes, leads a nice, calm, steady life as though he knows precisely where he's going. . . . When he asked me to marry him, I thought it over for a day or two and finally I decided it ought to work out fine. After all, there's only one part of his life which is important to him and which I don't give a damn for —this mystical bit—and he's never tried to convert me or even done the indirect things like leaving leaflets around for me to read. Far as he's concerned, it's so transparently right, so self-evident, he can wait for other people to catch up with him."

"I think that's an arrogant standpoint," Colin said when she paused to sip her beer.

"Arrogant? Oh, *yes!* That's why I'm on my own this afternoon—that's what we had a row about. He insisted I must go with him to some big gathering at their temple, or church, or whatever you call it. It's a curtain raiser to a huge international rally tomorrow in Washington Square. And I said no. Thinking he'd just shrug, the way he generally does. But instead of that, he started yelling at me!"

She shook her head, looking bewildered. "It's so unlike him! Since we arrived, he's changed—no, that's wrong. More: He's *been* changed. By meeting the people he came to see. I can't describe it exactly, but . . . Oh, it's as though he's desperately excited for the first time in his life, and being the sort of controlled person he is, he doesn't know how to let it show. Does that make any sort of sense?"

"I think so," Colin said with a nod. "But of course since I don't know him, I can't—"

"Know him!" Her voice was almost a cry. "Colin, nor do I! And doesn't it make me sound like the worst kind of fool to admit that I've married him and haven't bothered to find out about what he regards as more important than anything in the world?"

"But surely—" Colin began, thinking of the magazine he had seen at Larry's apartment.

"Oh!" She brushed the air as though to slap his words aside. "Of course I know a bit about it, but only a bit. A snatch here and there, what stuck in my mind when I picked up one of his books out of sheer curiosity. And— Oh my God! Colin, *what's that?*"

She pointed through the window, across the street, and he whipped his head around and saw—

But providentially a car rolled by a second later. Nonetheless he shivered, and not because the air conditioning was turned to its coldest setting.

"Didn't you see it?" she cried, clutching his hand.

"See what?" he parried by reflex, his voice thick and his throat tight with tension.

No, I can't have seen anything. I mustn't have!

And yet in London he and Vanessa had shared something that was not of the commonplace world. . . .

Stop it! Stop, stop!

"Something that moved," Vanessa said. "Something that wasn't—well—wasn't quite a *thing*. . . ."

A formless movement. That was what he had called it to himself when he was fighting to find his way back to sanity. Nothing there, and yet—movement! Illusion. Must have been. The doctors said so. And here again it could be illusion, a trick of hot air rising off the sidewalk, refraction of light by a car's exhaust, something—anything!

He said in the steadiest tone he could muster, "Vanessa, there's nothing to be scared of."

"Oh, how completely right you are!" a girl's voice said loudly from an adjacent table. Jolted, Colin swung around and found himself being beamed at by a range of teeth like tombstones, topped by green cat's-eye glasses and surrounded by a square-cut pageboy bob.

Rising, the girl approached. "Indeed there's nothing to be afraid of," she went on. "Not when you've found the true meaning of life—not when you've discovered a creed which doesn't abuse your reason with the dogmas of religion but backs its claims with actual *proof!*"

Vanessa, Colin saw, had turned perfectly white.

Fumbling in a purse, the girl produced a garish leaflet. "Here's a schedule of our meetings," she said. "There's one tonight, and tomorrow we're holding a big rally. How lucky that I caught you—I was just leaving! Do come and listen to what we have to say. I'm sure someone who can make the remark you just made is looking for our message and only needs to be told that it's there. And by the way, it's knowledge that moves mountains, you know, not faith."

With a final flash of her enormous and extremely white teeth, she walked out.

"Who the hell was she?" Colin demanded, tossing the leaflet aside.

"A Real Truther. That's the cult Larry belongs to," Vanessa said. "He's staging the open-air rally she mentioned."

"And what in hell is the Real Truth?"

"If you can imagine such a thing," she replied wearily, "it's an anthropocentric religion. Claims that the mind of man is the greatest thing in the universe, and anything you can conceive you can achieve. That's one of their favorite slogans, by the way."

"I don't believe I ever heard of it."

"I'm not surprised. It appeals to a special kind of person: intellectually overdeveloped, emotionally underdeveloped." She interrupted herself with a harsh laugh. "Sounds as though I'm cut out for it, hm? But in fact I'm not, though it suits Larry to a T— Oh, Colin, I could hate myself for saying that! Because he has been very kind to me!"

Privately Colin wondered how selfless that kindness had been; however, he was reluctant to pass judgment on someone he hadn't met.

"You mean they literally worship man?" he said, and on her nod continued, searching for distraction: "Well, I guess something like that was bound to crop up. J. B. S. Haldane once suggested that if at the end of last century someone had founded a religion whose dogmas included the existence of the ether and mechanistic causal physics, he'd have held up modern science for who knows how long. And did you ever read Eimar O'Duffy's *Spacious Adventures of the Man in the Street*? That was in antiscience satire where it was obligatory to believe that all anthropoid apes climbed trees ten feet tall to escape saber-toothed tigers, so only the ones with the shortest tails evolved into human beings."

He had hoped for a smile at the grand absurdity of the image. But she was paying him no attention. Almost petrified, she was staring toward the street again.

"Look!" she said in a strangled voice. "Coming this way! It is —I swear it is! The man who called himself Kolok!"

V

Colin's heart began to pound with a beat like the tread of a firing party walking down a long echoing passage toward his own execution. Yes, it was Kolok, as he had been in London —even to the long dark overcoat, so incongruous on the hot New York street that it was attracting the attention of passers-by. He might have skipped the intervening weeks and stepped directly from that to this moment of time.

He was heading straight for them, yet somehow he seemed not to be looking at them or even at the window through which they must be plainly visible. More, Colin felt, he was *listening*—and to some sound fainter than the roar of traffic.

A car braked to avoid him, its driver shouting a curse, but he took no notice. His attention was on something that must be more important than his personal safety.

At the base of the window, within reach of Colin's arm but for the glass, something moved—or rather, there was motion. His scalp prickled. Once more he was too late when he tried to focus on it. But it had been the same as whatever Vanessa had thought she saw a few minutes ago, the same as whatever he, too, had seemed to see during his breakdown. . . .

He wanted to rise and run, yet at the same time he was afraid that if he went on to the street, he might find that what he hoped might be imaginary was not.

He was quaking when Kolok stormed in at the door, and as though up to this point he had been relying on something other than his eyesight, he seemed to switch from one mode of attention to another and halted by their table. The blank expression vanished from his heavy-jowled face, to be replaced with a look of near-terror, and when he spoke, his voice was virtually a moan.

"Why did you come together again?"

"Who are you?" Vanessa demanded shrilly. "What do you want?"

"To warn you! I told you before—you must not be together anywhere! If you split up, it is more difficult for them, and I'll do all I can to stop them driving you to the same place a third time. But they have succeeded twice already, and now one of them has you in sight continually!"

Colin felt a helpless dizzying sensation that he recalled from the onset of his breakdown: an impression that no matter how hard he tried to convince himself that he was prey to terror bred in his own brain, he would never be able to overcome his fear again. Real or not real, he was at its mercy.

Struggling to break loose from a mental spider web, he heard Vanessa framing the questions he wanted to but could not utter.

"Who are 'they'? And who are *you?*"

"I'm a friend, perhaps the only friend you have," Kolok asserted meaninglessly. "And 'they'—they are the people who brought you together in London and now again here: the people who ruined your lives, destroyed your career, destroyed Colin's hope of marriage, who stop at nothing to get you at their mercy. When you come together, it is like completing a whole, and you release vast powers!"

"No," Colin heard himself say. He had not intended to speak, but he was driven to it. "This is delirium. No one persecuted me and deliberately ruined my life. I thought someone had, but it was due to paranoia. The doctors said so, and I must believe them."

"Forget the doctors!" Kolok rapped. "They didn't know what I know!"

Colin laughed aloud, sarcastically, and glanced around in the hope that someone, some stranger at another table, might bring reinforcements to prop his sagging confidence. But none of the other customers was paying attention; raised voices typically implied an argument, and it was best not to become involved in a private quarrel.

And even Vanessa would not take his side, he realized with sudden dismay. For she was asking still another question.

"What are the things that move just before you can look straight at them?"

"Trnak!" was Kolok's astonishing reply. "But so long as you are apart, they cannot harm you. It's only if you stay together that they'll close in."

"Now just a moment!" Colin exclaimed. "You're talking as though those—those moving shadows really exist!"

"What more proof do you need than what you have?" Kolok snapped. "Vanessa has seen them—you've seen them—and I have a name to label them by!"

"But—but . . .!" Colin's mouth was suddenly very dry, but his mind was calm, and he was able to reason again. "Let's get this perfectly straight. You're saying they are real."

"Perhaps not with the reality which you normally—" Kolok began, and with a crowing laugh Colin cut him short.

"I don't know who you are or how you tracked us down,

but I know this! I never want to see you again or hear your lunatic babbling—is that clear? Vanessa, let's get out of earshot of this madman!"

He jumped up, flung coins on the table, and seized her by the arm.

Face beaded with sweat, Kolok said, "I'll do my best to hold them back. But at the very least go north—you must go north!"

Colin looked at Vanessa steadily. "He's talking about what I know I saw when I was crazy," he said. "Are you going to do as he tells you, or are you coming with me?"

She hesitated only fractionally; then she was ahead of him and out the door.

Whereupon he took her by the hand and turned right: southward.

She hung back. "Colin, he told us to go north!"

"And are you going to obey?" he barked. "Because I'm not!"

In the alley next to the Firenze, where a sign pointed to Johnny Feen's Coffeehouse, something moved without movement. The hairs rose on Colin's neck, but when he looked again, there was only a young black man holding the door for a girl to pass.

"Colin, are you ill?" she demanded, having to run to keep pace with him.

"I don't know. I hope not. I remember what it was like to be ill. I mean crazy." He was glancing from side to side, but everything he saw was commonplace. "A sense of being watched. Things moving that I never quite saw clearly. The world turning into a horrible, soft, plastic stage set. And this isn't like that." They had to halt for a red light; he took her arm in eager fingers, grasping it as though its solidity were an anchor for him. "Tell me that it's not. Tell me this is New York, a real city full of real people!"

"Yes, of course it is!" she cried.

Yet London is a real city, too, and there we walked through an impossible door . . .

"I told you," he said, using his voice to drown the creeping tide of terror in his mind. "They gave me drugs, and the things went away. I'm not going to let them come back. I'm not— I'm *not!*"

She had no more words to offer, but she put her arm around his shoulder, and little by little as they walked along, the wave of pure panic died away. Until at last he was able to take a new grip on himself, raise his head, give a tolerable imitation of a smile, and say: "Vanessa, I'm very sorry. More sorry than I can possibly explain. But whoever and whatever that man Kolok is, he reminds me of something I hoped to forget for good and all."

"Don't I remind you of it, too?" she whispered. "I was with you when he first appeared."

"I can only half believe in you," he answered. "You're the only good thing that ever turned up in my visions."

There was a brief silence. At last she shrugged and glanced around. "Where are we?" she said. "We've walked a pretty long way."

"Oh, we're—" Colin began, and broke off. He thought he knew Greenwich Village well, but this spot he didn't recognize: a small square with sad-looking trees in the middle across which numerous people were walking as though bound for a common destination.

He felt a tap on his shoulder and swung around.

It was the girl in green-framed glasses who had accosted them in the Firenze.

"So you did decide to come," she said simply. "I'm glad."

She passed on, leaving Vanessa staring after her in horror.

"This must be Mann Square!" she forced out. "It's where the Real Truthers have their headquarters—yes, look!"

She pointed. Between the trees Colin saw a corner building, formerly used as a store, whose display windows had been painted over from inside. Across them, foot-high gilt letters proclaimed that this was "The First New York Seat of the Real Truth."

"Are all these people coming to a meeting?" he murmured. "Why, there must be hundreds of them!"

"Larry said the cult is getting very strong here," Vanessa answered, locking her hands together so that the knuckles glistened white. "Oh, Colin, this is terrible! Look at their faces!"

"What's wrong with their faces? They look like ordinary people, don't they?"

"Can't you see how empty—?" She checked with a sigh. "No, I suppose not. It must all be in my mind. You're right: ordinary people."

Colin looked at them again and found no reason to change his opinion. Most of them were young, but there were a sprinkling of the middle-aged, and also a number of elderly women —just what he would have expected.

"What else do you know about their beliefs?" he demanded. "What's so special that it can bring them out in such numbers?"

"Oh . . ." Vanessa swallowed. "There's something about a Messiah figure—they call him the Perfect Man. The idea is that by concentrating hard they'll think him into existence. And he'll have all the psi powers, read minds and foresee the future and move objects without touching them and the rest of that rubbish. . . . Colin, it's no use asking me. I never let Larry talk to me about it because I don't hold with that sort of thing."

That was a different way of putting it—"never *let* him talk about it"—and Colin suspected it was nearer the truth. Still, he wasn't entitled to complain about people who hid behind self-defensive white lies; he'd done it so often himself. . . .

"Is Larry high up in the organization?"

"Pretty high, I suppose. I mean, they must think a lot of him to bring him over from London, just to devise their—their whatever-you-call-it. Liturgy? Ritual? And speak of the devil."

"What?"

"There he is. He's spotted us. He's coming this way. I want to run like hell, and it's far too late."

A cheerful voice rang out: "Vanessa, darling! Changed your mind, I see—and I'm so glad!"

Larry Adderley was lean, fortyish, handsome in a slightly weak-chinned way. His hair was fair and curly, and he wore casual clothes that were a trifle too exquisite, and two rings and an enormous matching watch.

Vanessa suffered him to embrace her fleetingly, detached herself, and gestured at Colin.

"Larry, this is a friend I bumped into in the Village, Colin Hooper. Colin, I've been telling you about my husband."

"How do you do?" Larry said, not visibly pleased at meeting his wife here with a stranger after he himself had failed to persuade her to come along. "Well, you are coming in for the service, aren't you, now you're here? It starts in five minutes, and there are some fascinating rumors going around."

"About what?" Colin said.

"About the arrival of the Perfect Man—what else?" Larry took Vanessa's arm and urged her proprietorially along with the rest of the crowd, and Colin tagged behind. After the shock he had undergone at the Firenze, after the near-renewal of his breakdown that had impelled him to walk so far and so fast in the direction opposite to what Kolok wanted, he had no mental energy left to wonder about what he was being let in for.

Passively waiting for a chance to file into the temple, or

whatever, with everybody else, he found himself looking at a street name on a lamp standard. Yes, it said, "Mann Square."

Surely the symbolism was a little crude?

VI

Judging by the fact that, as Vanessa had remarked, Larry had been brought clear from England to supervise the Washington Square rally tomorrow—and what better expert could a modern religion call on than a movie director when it wanted to stage an impressive public service?—he must indeed belong to the upper echelons of the cult. Right up to the last moment, therefore, Colin vaguely hoped that he and Vanessa might be left alone, might find the chance to sneak back out.

Not so. Larry, chatting away about the coming of the Perfect Man and occasionally greeting friends with a cheerful shout, stayed with them, plainly determined to sit through the ceremony in their company. Aching with unaccountable apprehension, Colin allowed himself to be ushered into the meeting hall.

Two complete stories of this and the adjacent building must have been hollowed out to create it. It was bare but not stark; there was carpet everywhere, and concentric seats, luxuriously padded, ringed a circular dais on which a single screened light shone from the center of the ceiling. The dais bore a pair of statues carved by a master: a man and a woman alike gazing upward in attitudes that implied aspiration, indomitability, achievement.

In spite of himself, Colin was impressed. Even though the service itself might be pure rigmarole, he felt he could endure it with those magnificent sculptures to admire.

When virtually all the seats were full, faint music resounded from above, and the lights grew dim. Simultaneously they changed color, except the one in the center. The walls seemed to vanish into a vast blue distance. The resemblance was so unexpected that the process was half complete before he was able to round on Vanessa, an exclamation rising to his lips.

But Larry had been watching him and hissed an order to be quiet.

Feeling like an animal in a trap, he turned to see if there was any way out, but there were a dozen people between him and the nearest aisle, and all were leaning forward with expressions of idiot adoration, awaiting the commencement of their act of worship. Now he knew what Vanessa had seen in the faces she had called "empty."

It was too late now, though. He must go through with it.

A voice boomed from nowhere like the note of a bronze gong. It said: "THINK!"

Behind the word, unspoken, was implied contempt for those who did not use their minds, the one thing that set men apart from beasts, the most vital force in the cosmos. Colin heard gasps from all around, as though a hundred people were yielding to orgasm.

The statue of a man turned and looked over the audience. It was no longer a statue. It *was* a man, handsome as a god, clad in a long robe that swirled out as he moved.

"KNOW YOURSELVES!"

A sob from somewhere in this blue infinity.

"Remember that you create the universe," said the man. "And what you have created, you control!"

Behind him the statue of a woman turned into a globe of spiraling light, and it snatched at Colin's mind and flung him into another mode of being.

Later, he could not recapture what he had thought, what he had been shown. He had the merest impressions, more fleeting than the memory of a dream. He felt that he had looked into the heart of a sun and unveiled the secret of its billion-year glory; into the seed of a man and surveyed the history-shaking path of his descendants; into the depths of oceans, the void of space, the gulfs of time. He knew he was master over millions who owed him only love in return; he imagined that the answer to the riddle of the universe lay in his grasp; he believed it lay shining on his palm, but when he closed his fingers, he encountered only the smooth flesh of Vanessa's arm.

Struggling not to return to consciousness, like a man who has seen paradise in a vision, he found he could not avoid opening his eyes. Beyond the people separating him from the aisle, a man stood making urgent gestures. Kolok! Or at any rate his twin—fantastically clothed. Yet in no wise strangely. Properly! That floor-long blue robe so heavily crusted with golden symbols that its weight seemed to bow his shoulders was more right for him than ordinary clothing, and that guess Colin had made about his hair was justified, for an oddly formed gold and white cap exactly covered the unshaved area of his scalp.

With a commanding wave of both hands, he fixed Colin's attention, and that was welcome. Up there, Colin knew from the corner of his eye, the deceitful spiral of light was still spinning, still pouring forth its message of paradise. And it seemed that he was the only person in the hall, save Kolok, who was free of its enchantment for the moment. Even Larry, even Vanessa, were still trapped: Larry with his mouth so slackly open that a stream of saliva was running down his chin, Vanessa ungracefully sprawled across her seat. Their eyes were wide but saw nothing except the whirling whiteness.

"Come!" Kolok whispered sibilantly. "If you had only done as I told you. . . ! Still, it is not quite too late, even now. Wake her, make her come with you! If either of you remains to the end of the service, they will achieve resonance, and the way will open—so be quick!"

Having no faintest idea what Kolok was talking about, but convinced after his exposure to the vision of the Real Truth that it was more addictive and more delightful than any drug, Colin shook Vanessa by the shoulder.

She stirred and gave a little moan: "Leave me alone!"

He refused. He had learned from bitter experience how tempting it could be to abandon all hope, to sink into the slough of permanent insanity, and it was that same temptation he had recognized during the beginning of this—this service, if that was the right name for it. He twisted her head around so that instead of gazing at the white spiral she was looking toward Kolok, who held up both hands in front of his face, and somehow that broke the grip imprisoning her mind.

She stood up uncertainly, and Colin urged her to pick her way over the tangled legs and feet of the other worshipers until they were in the aisle at Kolok's side.

"Now you know how the adepts of the Real Truth recruit their followers," Kolok said softly. "At last you have seen what there is to be afraid of. Perhaps next time you will heed my warnings!"

"But I saw—" Vanessa began in a near whimper.

"You saw lies!" Kolok was whispering, but the sincerity of his manner loaded the words with more force than a shout.

"You saw illusion! Never a hint of the eternal enslavement of the soul which is the doom the Perfect Man will bring to Earth!"

Before Colin could ask for an explanation, a sound rasped through the blue mist: something heavy and badly oiled being forced back in reluctant grooves. Kolok whirled.

"They're coming! Follow me and be quick!"

He headed for the entrance, Vanessa and Colin at his heels.

"No, too late," he said, stopping suddenly dead. "Under the dais, then—there are steps. It's the only way. I'll try and confuse them, but I cannot promise more! *Run!*"

In the mist, as though solidifying out of air, there were blacknesses too vague to call shapes: movement without any *thing* moving. Colin's nerves stretched past the breaking point. He caught Vanessa's hand and dived for the side of the dais where Kolok pointed.

There was a dark opening. They stumbled into it and found the promised steps, leading downward—not that it mattered where they led, so long as it was away from the hall of blue mist. A more welcoming light gleamed at the bottom of them, yellow, like candle flame, and they came gasping into a passage hewed out of stone, here forming a right angle of which one arm led ahead, the other left.

Sounds of tramping feet and raised voices came from the branch ahead. They dodged to the left, frantically racing into twilight.

After a hundred yards, or two hundred, they encountered a mystery: A line of vivid blue paint was splashed across the floor, and symbols of the same color smeared the walls. They were meaningless to Colin; even so, intuition warned him of the need for caution. He reached out an arm across the line and groped in the air, suspiciously, as though in search of an unseen barrier.

"They're coming after us!" Vanessa cried. "Why did you stop?"

"I—I don't know. A feeling . . . But we must go on."

He took her arm, and they rushed onward, and five paces beyond the line, they fell.

It was as though they tumbled as far as Satan cast into the pit—fell through interstellar space from one sun to another, driven by the whiplashes of light—and yet it lasted between one step and the next, and the solid floor was there to meet their soles when they set down their feet again.

So, too, was a man whom they had not seen one pace ago: fat, and with a dimpled face coarsened by rich living. He wore a robe similar to Kolok's, though the golden symbols embroidered on it were much sparser. He wasted one second on not believing his eyes.

During that second Colin decided that they must trust Kolok, who had called himself the only friend they had. With ferocity he did not know was in him he clamped a hand over that blubber-lipped mouth and with the fingers of the other probed fat dewlaps for a stranglehold. He ignored Vanessa's half-weeping cries at his back, just as he ignored the fat man's attempts to struggle free, and after a short eternity the popping eyes closed, the full weight leaned limply on his arm.

He let the fat man slump to the floor.

"Colin, why did you have to do that?" Vanessa moaned. "Now they'll come after us, and—"

"They're after us already!" he snapped. "I don't know why, but Kolok seems to, and for a change I'm taking his advice. I wish I'd taken it before—we might not have stumbled into this nightmare! Come along!"

He urged her onward, and she came unresisting. Ahead, there was a junction like the one they had left behind. And a flight of steps like the ones they had come down. No!

More than just *like*. Identical. With a blur of bluish luminous mist at the top of them.

"We're—we're back where we started!" Vanessa whispered.

"We can't be!" Colin declared. And yet the similarity was total, as though they were seeing in a mirror the place where they had entered this passage. Yes, in a mirror, for here the passage branched the other way. . . .

He said so, excitedly, and added, "Perhaps this is a way out! Let's see!"

"Colin, be careful!"

"Yes, of course!"

But he was feeling lightheaded now. A kind of crazy confidence had taken possession of his mind. During the initial stages of his breakdown he had been aware that things were invading his world that could not possibly be real, yet he had been unable to escape them. When the—what was the word Kolok had used?—when the *trnak* had appeared beyond the window of the bar where they were sitting, when Kolok had arrived full of his incomprehensible frantic warnings, he had yielded to the same kind of terror, fearing that the world everyone else inhabited would be snatched away from him. But this was solid; this *was* real, no matter how illogical or inexplicable it might be. The relief of discovering that a real place could be as fantastic as his worst hallucinations had armored him against the urge to run into a corner and hide his head.

Slowly he mounted the steps. No formless black nonshapes gathered in the gloom. No fat men, gaudy in robes of blue and gold, stood waiting in ambush. Unmolested, they came to the top of the flight and found—

A dais from beneath whose base they were emerging. White light shed from above. All around, concentric rows of seats that held people slumped in a hypnotic stupor.

VII

"It's impossible!" Vanessa whispered from the verge of tears.

"Do the Real Truthers have two temples in New York?" Colin suggested. The shock of apparently finding that they were back at their starting point, after he had reviewed all the reasons for believing the contrary, had hit him like a douche of cold water. An hour ago he had been prey to irrational terror; a minute ago, to irrational confidence. Now he was poised between the two, and a steely clarity pervaded his mind.

"No, I'm sure Larry would have told me—he's boasted often enough about how many they've set up in a mere two years, and there's one in London, one in New York, one in . . . Colin, look at their *clothes!*"

His eyes adjusting to the blueness afresh, being very careful not to look at the whirling white spiral that dominated the temple here as well as there—whatever "here" and "there" might mean—Colin complied. In the front row of seats, perhaps five paces from where they stood, were half a dozen people: a stout woman in an ankle-length coat with five big horn buttons, a youth in a sort of tunic and leggings fastened with brass hasps and a rakish beret sliding down now over his right ear, a pretty girl in a gown with several layered capes around her shoulders, a man of middle age in a comfortable-looking quilted coat, and a boy and girl of about eight or ten in identical strap-fastened coats without the quilting. Nowhere in sight was there an ordinary suit or a dress of the kind that girls were wearing this summer in New York. Moreover, the garments of men and women alike had a peasant-coarse appearance, as though they were cut from a fabric as rough as sacking.

"Where are we?" Vanessa muttered.

"I've no idea," Colin answered heavily. "But we must be a hell of a long way from Greenwich Village!"

"We'd better go back, then! If—if we can go back!"

He didn't respond at once. He was thinking of the falling sensation that had overtaken them between one step and the next. Had that sense of vast distances been real? Had they in some weird fashion actually stepped from their familiar world into some other, similar world where people also worshiped the Perfect Man but had no clothing better than this ugly homespun? How? How?

If only Kolok could have come with us instead of staying behind to confuse the mysterious "them"!

Totally at a loss, he glanced down the steps under the dais. Perhaps Vanessa was right. If they went back, though they would risk running into someone who had found the body of the fat man, they might be able to regain New York. To stay here, not even knowing where "here" might be, was infinitely the more dangerous course.

"Yes, let's turn back," he muttered, and caught Vanessa's hand.

But on the second step downward there was movement half-seen at the corner of his eye, and something took hold of them in a grip less flexible than iron. As though reacting to an unheard order, four men tramped stolidly into view from the side branch of the passage below the steps.

Wanting to shout, to scream, to tear and smash, Colin stood helpless in the clutch of a black form neither solid nor hard yet immovably rigid. He could not even turn his head to see Vanessa; the force permitted him breath and the blinking of his eyes, nothing more.

At the head of the group of four was a self-important man in another of the blue gold-embroidered robes. The symbols must indicate some sort of rank structure, Colin reasoned. In which case, Kolok . . .

But there was no chance to speculate now.

The blue-robed man looked the captives over with evident satisfaction, then nodded at the trio accompanying him. All three were big men, dark-skinned, bearded, in rough leather jerkins, homespun breeches, high boots, and belts made of braided rope. The one who seemed to be a leader, perhaps a sergeant, bore a short sword, the others cudgels of bog oak; all wore polished wooden casques.

The man in blue said something in a high voice: an order. The language was completely unfamiliar to Colin. The men with cudgels promptly hoisted him and Vanessa up on their shoulders as casually as though they were picking up potato sacks.

It was frustrating as well as humiliating to be carried off, writhing impotently against bonds of blackness, but Colin relaxed at last and concentrated on noticing where they were being taken. If by some miracle they broke free, they must be able to retrace their steps to the dais and the underground passage that was their only link with the normal Earth.

They were borne along an aisle flanked by members of the stupefied congregation and through wide double doors of carved wood guarded by sentries who bowed and extended their cudgels on their open palms in something between a salute and a gesture of submission. The robed man acknowledged their tribute with a curt nod.

Beyond the doors they entered a high-roofed passageway splendidly ornamented with more carvings, including larger-than-life statues in polished stone. That apart, the corridor was stark—almost primitive. Bare planks boomed under the soldiers' boots. What light there was came from windows innocent of glass, beside each of which hung a heavy shutter on wooden peg hinges. Every few paces a sconce, at head height, held a crude torch ready to be lit when darkness fell.

The glimpses he caught of the outside world showed him only the wall of a timber building, a patch of dark green grass, a few shrubs and trees. It was apparently, though, about the same season and time of day in New York: summer evening.

The same time as in New York! Where the hell are we? Who are these people? How could a run of a few hundred yards down an underground passage bring us to a completely different world?

The questions tormented Colin's brain, but in the grip of the black nothingness he could neither voice nor answer them.

The clump of the soldiers' boots and the hushing of the sandals that the robed man wore sent echoes running ahead of them to a second and finer pair of doors. Here guards in rows of three with pikes eight feet long raised and lowered their weapons by pairs before and behind, so that they had to filter through. On every face Colin saw a uniform expression of grim menace.

The doors were swung back, and the robed man shouted something ringing and respectful, then dropped to his face on the floor. A pace behind, the one whom Colin thought of as a sergeant did the same, while the two common soldiers who carried himself and Vanessa sketched an awkward dip with one knee, afraid of letting fall their burdens.

They were in an oblong room, perhaps a hundred feet by sixty. Plaintive music resounded; tapestries, gaudy with red and yellow and blue, adorned the walls; the floor was strewn with a layer of dried herbs that gave off a sweet scent when crushed by the weight of a foot. Around the walls stood knots of men and women, mostly in the ubiquitous blue robes, but some in similar garments of green or brown and a few in quilted coats over leggings. Slender, bronzed men wearing only breechcloths carried trays of beaten brass laden with bowls of food and cups of liquor from one such cluster to the next.

Opposite the doors by which they had been brought in, a man in a robe of gold sat negligently on a wide soft couch. On cushions at his feet reclined two plump but not unattractive girls wearing golden girdles, golden sandals, and nothing else except hair ornaments and a plenitude of eye kohl and lip rouge. Behind the couch a group of blue-robed men looked coldly on the newcomers. One of them called out, and the soldiers moved forward until at length Colin found himself and Vanessa set on their feet, as though they were Real Truth statues being placed on their plinths, facing the contemptuous gaze of the man in gold. He had a heavy, powerful face with a sensual mouth and beetling brows; his hair was carefully dressed to fall on his nape in thick, regular waves; he was clean-shaven except for a fringe of whiskers on each of his cheeks, aligned on the corners of his nose, and his eyes were green, the color of the sea.

Apparently very proud of himself, the leader of their captors bowed with a flourish and began to speak. He must, Colin guessed, be boasting about how cleverly he had caught these intruders. But he had scarcely uttered twenty words before the face of the man in gold changed as though a light had been turned off behind it. The air suddenly burned, as from the physical embodiment of abstract rage, and the music stopped instantly. Everyone in the hall uttered a unison gasp—

And the man in the blue robe doubled up, writhing, and began to vomit blood.

Matter-of-factly, two of the bronzed men in breechcloths

dragged him away by the corners of his robe. Terrified, the sword-bearing sergeant was on his knees, knocking his forehead against the floor and crying out in a pleading tone, but the man in gold favored him with no more than an insult, and he rose and backed off to one side, trembling and gulping.

The man in gold made a beckoning movement without looking to see if it was obeyed; his eyes were fixed on Colin and Vanessa. Abruptly the restraint was gone from them. Colin almost fell down with the shock of being released. He wanted to seize Vanessa and comfort her, but he felt it safer to stand rock-still for fear some ill-judged movement might visit him also with that ghastly inexplicable punishment.

In response to the beckoning there tottered forward a figure in dark green. Colin was unable to decide whether it was man or woman, for it was very old and only a few wisps of white hair clung to its wrinkled scalp.

It halted beside the man in gold and spoke in a surprisingly resonant tone.

"Since this poor thing is acquainted with your intolerably barbaric tongue, I shall have to make use of her to communicate with you." A mocking expression on the face of the man in gold accompanied the statement.

Colin hunted for his own voice, but he seemed to have lost it beyond recall.

"I who honor you by addressing you am called Telthis! Remember that! It is a name you will have cause to know well when I am lord of your world as well as this one. It was opportune of you to find your way here; you have saved me an effort which of course I could well have made, but which would have been somewhat tedious."

"Your world as well as this one"? What kind of crazy gibberish is that?

Though—where are we? This can't be any place on Earth!

Some hint of his thoughts, Colin assumed, must have shone on his face, for Telthis gave an amused chuckle, and the old crone spoke again.

"I sense you are angry, Colin Hooper! Seethe away—it's the most you can do! Neither you nor anyone else in your world of cripples can harm a hair of my head. Of my goodness I will treat you well, for I find you convenient to my purpose, but never think to read in that a sign of weakness. I will give you proof of the powers I possess, so that you may understand how feeble you are, and all those like you. Watch!"

He jerked his head. One of the bronze-skinned menservants came forward and stood passively facing the couch. Telthis leaned forward, elbows on knees, face in a frown of concentration. Hurriedly the girls at his feet moved aside and clung to one another.

For seconds nothing seemed to be happening. Then the bronzed man screamed. A column of flame shot up from his breechcloth and his hair. A wave of heat, fierce as the opening of a furnace, slapped their faces. Oily black smoke rose to stain the ceiling. Vanessa gave a wordless moan, and Colin bent double, retching in horror.

"You have no stomach for such sights?" the crone boomed in Telthis's words. "Then remember what I can do when next I call you to me! Take them away!"

The soldiers, with briskness that suggested they were glad to leave the presence of their sadistic overlord, pinioned Colin and Vanessa with skillful hands and force-marched them from the hall. One last insane fact struck Colin as he was pushed through the door: The tapestries on the wall had changed since their arrival and were still changing, like slow, slow cinema pictures.

VIII

They were shoved stumbling into a room so narrow it might better be termed a cell; it contained a rough bed, a wooden stool, and a slop bucket, and the walls were of dank gray stone. Bars blocked the one high window, beyond which the smeared clouds of sunset loured redder than blood. Behind them there was the grating noise of bolts being forced down ungreased slides.

The instant they were alone Vanessa turned blindly to him and hid her face against his shoulder, sobbing in deep throat-wrenching gusts bred of naked terror. Mechanically stroking her hair, Colin stared blankly at the window and let her recover in her own time, wishing more than a little that he could do the same.

When he felt the sobs abate, he guided her gently to the bed and sat her down on the hard mattress. It felt as though it was stuffed with straw, or perhaps rushes, and it was damp.

"He did do it, didn't he?" she mumbled. "Telthis, I mean. He wished the man to burn, and he did, didn't he? But how—*how?*"

Colin shook his head and uttered some meaningless phrase of reassurance.

"And he made the old woman speak to us, didn't he?" Vanessa went on.

"It seemed like it."

"But it's impossible! Colin, I can't believe it—I must be dreaming, or insane!"

"No, I'm afraid this isn't a dream. It's too damned solid. Too real." He looked around the shadowy confines of the cell; sunset glow was reflected in a single square red patch on the upper edge of the barred door, but apart from that the gloom was oppressive. "Let's think through what we've learned so far, and maybe it'll make a bit more sense."

At least it might help to stave off despair.

But he thought it wiser not to utter that dangerous word.

Taking a tight grip on herself, she nodded and clicked open her purse, which she had managed to cling to in spite of everything. From it she produced cigarettes, a book of matches, a handkerchief with which to dab her tear-swollen eyes. Lighting a cigarette was satisfactorily commonplace, a link with the ordinary world; Colin felt ridiculously better when he had drawn the first puff.

"Telthis," he said musingly. "Lord of what he calls 'this world.' If that's true, they breed dictators here who would make our worst tyrants look like naughty children!"

"But where is 'this world'?" she asked simply.

"Well, one thing's certain. It isn't twentieth-century Earth."

"And yet it's—it's right next door!" She shook her head. "And that temple in New York must have been modeled on the one we found when we . . . What did we do?"

"Came over," Colin grunted. "Lord knows how."

"Do you suppose the Real Truthers know about this other world? Do you suppose someone like Larry might be able to come hunting for us?" She sounded as though she was trying to force herself to believe the impossible. "How long have we been on—on this side?"

He held up his wrist to catch the slanting sunlight.

"Funny," he said after a moment. "It says ten after six. But the service in the temple started at six, and we've been here much longer than ten minutes, I'm sure of that."

"Your watch stopped before," Vanessa said. "In the room off Tippet Lane."

He nodded, his face drawn and anxious. "What about yours?"

"I don't have it with me. I put it in for repair in London. They said they couldn't find a thing wrong with it except that it doesn't run. So they sent it back to the factory in Switzerland."

Breathing hard, Colin cast around in his mind for something else to say. He wanted to think about anything rather than this crazy otherwhere ruled by a supernaturally talented barbarian despot and policed by club-carrying soldiers in leather jerkins. But he had to concentrate. There did remain the slim chance of spotting a clue they'd overlooked.

"Oh, no!" Vanessa cried out suddenly.

"What's wrong?" he exclaimed.

"I can feel myself itching—there must be fleas in this mattress!"

"Here, let me see!"

She jumped up, and he produced the little flashlight that had proved so helpful in Tippet Lane. But when he pressed the switch, nothing happened.

Funny! It's less than a week since I put in a fresh cell.

"Sorry," he said, in as calm a tone as he could manage. "I must have forgotten to replace the battery. Let me have a match. And—hell, I should have thought of this before. They haven't taken anything away from us, not even your purse. We ought to go through what we have and see if there's anything that might help us escape."

"Escape?" she said bitterly. "What good would that do? We'd have to go back the way we came, and we'd be ambushed."

Before he could answer, there was an interruption. A spyhole opened in the thick door, and the curious eye of a soldier was set to it. It chanced that his gaze fell on Vanessa taking the last drag of her cigarette and breathing out a cloud of smoke that a gleam of sunlight turned to red.

The man exclaimed so loudly Colin thought of the tale of Walter Raleigh's servant who doused his master with a pail of water, thinking he was on fire because he had never seen tobacco pipes before. Bolts ground back; the door swung wide.

And there, pushing the soldier aside, was the last person they might have hoped to see, still in his blue robe and strange white and gold cap.

"Kolok!" Vanessa cried.

He pulled the door shut behind him, his face eloquent of fatigue. "Yes, indeed," he muttered. "Come for the final time to try and persuade you to save yourselves." He sat down on the wooden stool, spreading to either side the robe that suited him indefinably better than ordinary clothing. Of course, Colin thought, to him it was ordinary garb.

"Oh, you fools, you fools, to have delivered yourselves into the hands of Telthis!"

Colin bit back a resentful retort; argument would be a waste of time.

"I'd better start by shocking you into believing me—though I'm told Telthis has already shaken your skepticism," Kolok went on. "Watch this!"

He scowled with the same concentration Telthis had shown, and Colin's heart lurched. But the worst that happened was that the cigarette butt was twitched from his fingers by a bodiless force; Vanessa's purse tumbled across the bed of its own accord, the contents rattling; and lastly the stool, bearing Kolok, rose from the floor and could plainly be seen to float on nothing.

"I dare do nothing more spectacular," Kolok grunted. "They're afraid you may have powers yourselves, and they're bound to scan this cell pretty frequently. I can deceive these blockheaded guards"—with a jerk of his thumb at the door—"to the point where they won't even remember that I came here. But if a senior adept got wind of my presence . . . Incidentally, I've exterminated the fleas you were worried about. Have I finally convinced you?"

Shaking, Vanessa whispered, "Did you hypnotize us, or did you really float up off the floor?"

Kolok made an impatient gesture. "What does it matter? Our adepts gave up arguing about reality long ago. If something happens which all your senses confirm consistently, on which other observers equally agree, that's enough to work with. Take it as read that I 'really' floated. Now: Have you any idea where you are, how you came here, for what purpose?"

Colin shook his head. Throat dry, tongue thick, he forced out, "Only that we can't be anywhere on Earth—"

"Wrong. That's exactly where you are. Commonly this world is known as Troms, but it circles the same sun as Earth, and at the same distance. It has done so for the same period of time. It has the same continents and islands, and human beings live on it. But it and Earth are apart, as two sheets of paper are separated in a closed book—or, better, you might say it is distant in the direction which separates two copies of the same book."

Hazily, Colin muttered, "Fourth dimension?"

"Fifth—one not belonging to either Earth, yours or ours, but indispensable because it keeps them apart. Do you understand?"

"It's—it's the infinite universe concept," Vanessa ventured. "If the universe is infinite, it follows that somewhere there must be another world identical to ours."

Kolok shook his head. "Science in your world is far advanced over our own, yet somehow this idea seems to have been overlooked completely on your side. I've tried to relate your scientists' teachings to the knowledge garnered by our adepts, and they don't connect. . . . Still, I must try and make it clear. I'll give the explanation our best clairvoyants have compiled; like any hypothesis it serves as a guide for enlightened guesswork, if nothing more.

"I was just telling you that we do not know whether, when we cause an event to *seem* so, it *is* so. Our suspicion, however, is that the reality of the preanimate cosmos differed from the present reality. To put it in the most extreme terms, the universe may well be a figment of the minds of mankind. Certainly massed human minds constitute the only force known to be powerful enough to change it.

"You are to accept that long ago—perhaps ten, perhaps twelve thousand years—it *was* changed. I must think in your terms here, because our own cannot be translated with any precision. You would say, then, that a mutant woman was born with a genetic factor transmissible to both her sons and her daughters. It was due to—oh—a celestial accident. Radiation, maybe. It doesn't matter.

"But a savage tribe descended on the settlement where she lived and carried off one of her children, a baby daughter. Years later, the tribe which had been attacked retaliated, and when they were dividing up captured women among the victors, her son unknowingly chose his own sister.

"Their child had the power which I possess. As you would put it, the gene was latent and required inbreeding to bring it to the surface. What happened in your world, I don't know, but we presume that the fetus aborted, or the mother died, or —anyhow, something frustrated the boy from growing up to achieve the dominance which he enjoyed in ours. It is because in our history he did survive that although you are on the same island on the same planet the same distance from the same sun, you are not in a place called Manhattan, but in

Egla-Garthon, capital city of the dominion of Telthis, the ruler of the world."

"Literally?" Colin choked on the word.

"Yes, in every sense. I have not shown you a fraction of the power which millennia of training and study have evolved. Yet, it occurs to me, one piece of evidence is all around you. At this time of year, is it not unbearably hot and muggy in New York, while here it is tolerably cool?"

Colin started. "Yes! But I assumed it was because you don't have thousands of buildings with air conditioning here."

"Oh, indeed, that accounts for a part of it. But very little. It suits Telthis to remain here during the summer; therefore a few junior adepts are required to ensure that the temperature never exceeds what he regards as comfortable. Is that not indeed mastery of the world?" Kolok shook his head dolefully. "When the lightest whim of the mind can be translated directly into action at almost any distance, what need is there for tools and weapons? Naked and alone, Telthis could destroy a hundred armies."

Colin felt a shiver pass down his spine. What man, granted total power, could refrain from using it? And would not his first target inevitably be his fellow men?

"You seemed to imply," Vanessa said, so slowly it was as though she was afraid to hear the answer, "that we had been brought here for a purpose."

"I said you have not seen a fraction of the full power," Kolok replied obliquely. "With it, the gifted can sometimes spy a little into the future—though, as I said, the massed minds of humanity can change reality, so what's yet to come is malleable. Also, they can peer into the past, just as they can across oceans and into the bowels of the earth. And some can see a little in the fifth direction. Telthis is one who can. Telthis has the most complete armory of mental weapons ever wielded by one man—why else would he be ruler of the world?

"But he did not win this dominion for himself. He inherited it. And like anyone jealous of the shadow of his ancestors, he seeks new glories to add to theirs. One world at his beck and call is not enough. He is determined to add a second, and at this instant I can point to no reason and say with honesty, 'Therefore he will not succeed!' "

Somber-faced, he gave a sigh. "No, indeed. Your world, too, will shortly own the yoke of Telthis."

IX

They sat long in silence after that, the doom-laden words seeming to echo and re-echo as though they had been spoken in a vast empty hall instead of this narrow cell. At last Vanessa said, "But what does it have to do with *us?*"

"You carry, both of you, the genes which united in my world to produce Telthis and his—and *our*—ancestors."

"But—!" Together Colin and Vanessa half-rose from the foul straw mattress.

"Why should you find that surprising? Your scientists well know that a gene is a chemical message across time. Doubtless there are more bearers of it than just you two. Possibly there are millions by now. But . . .

"Oh, there is so much to explain! Bear with me, and remember that I've studied your world, while you know next to nothing about mine. Leave me to judge in what order the data will make most sense to you."

"I'm sorry," Colin muttered, and took Vanessa's hand. He felt her tremble.

"Well, then: Consider the difficulties Telthis faced in setting out to conquer another world. Only a few skilled adepts can even glimpse its existence, and the strain of thinking oneself into a frame of mind such that one can comprehend a world where everything is unlike what we regard as 'normal'—that, believe me, is near impossible. Yet Telthis wanted it done, so . . .

"Gradually it has become easier, as we've learned more of the other world. Projecting one's awareness into it is now far less formidable a task than it was when we began. But very shortly it became clear that without help from the other side, a physical crossing of the fifth-dimensional barrier was out of the question. It was here that Telthis showed a spark of true genius. He conceived the notion of matching his congregations of massed uniform minds with more, but in your world instead of ours.

"You have seen one such congregation. Apart from drugging people into obedience with delusions of omnipotence and omniscience, so vivid that the commoners live literally for nothing else, our services can be employed to reinforce a single thought, a single desire, projected by an adept. Local alterations of reality, as you've been shown, are within one man's scope. To affect a whole world you need perhaps ten thousand minds.

"Telthis set his adepts to scouring your world for people susceptible to mental influence. Some were found—as I've said, though the gene remains latent in your world, it's very widespread. In the minds he could influence, Telthis planted the urge to found a cult, to preach its creed, to raise money and build temples similar to ours, to recruit the congregations that ultimately would batter down the barrier from your side as well as ours.

"That was half the battle won. Shortly it became possible to achieve bodily transfer between the worlds—but still only master adepts could make the trip, and such progress was too slow for Telthis. He, of course, could have visited your world himself long ago, but he is determined that his first entry shall be as a conqueror, and your teeming billions are beyond even his fantastic capability. Had he crossed over with every last one of his finest adepts, he would still have risked exhaustion before the enslavement was complete. Therefore, he plans to take through an entire army, hordes of men—and women—without the faintest shadow of his mental power, simply to batter down resistance by brute force.

"Fuming with impatience, he sought some way to speed his plan, and then eventually the searchers who were hunting for susceptible minds in which to plant the vision of the Real Truth stumbled across two very extraordinary people. You!

"After thousands of years of mixing of the gene pool, two people had been born on opposite sides of the planet whose children—were they to meet and marry—would have the power-bestowing gene in full."

"Oh my God!" Vanessa said emptily. "It makes me feel like —like a ticking bomb!"

"Like a bomb?" Kolok echoed. "Very like! In you two the power is so close to fulfilment that even your coming together acts as a catalyst. Separate, you have no powers that show. Side by side, you are like uranium in one of your nuclear power stations. You are the channel for vast forces."

"But what kind of forces?" Vanessa demanded. "I mean, we can't float through the air or move things without touching them . . . can we?"

"You recall your meeting in a street called Tippet Lane? Then, for the first time without the aid of massed, hypnotized minds, physical transfer became possible between our worlds. The door of a prosaic storeroom became a gateway across a fifth-dimensional gulf. As I know well! For it was because you were still together, hours later, that I was able to use that road on which there was no rain. Do you remember?"

He searched their faces with keen, infinitely sad eyes.

"You're hinting," Colin said, "that we weren't brought together by chance. That Telthis planned our meeting!"

"Yes, he did. When you were located, you were deeply in love with a girl you meant to marry. You intended to settle down. Being of the temperament you are, you would no doubt have been a faithful husband. So Telthis—" A gesture with two fingers, like scissors closing.

"I can tell how angry that makes you," Kolok added apologetically. "Please master your emotions. It doesn't matter how it was done. It can't be set right. And we have little time to talk—so little time!"

Colin felt as though his heart had been ripped out and replaced by red-hot iron. But he held his tongue; only his nails dug pain-deep into his palms.

"The shock of that drove you for a while into a breakdown where attempts at contact from this side could be dismissed as hallucinations. You have powerful drugs in your world which screen out the transdimensional touch of even an advanced adept. Desperately Telthis awaited your recovery, but even when you left the hospital, it remained too dangerous to probe your mind directly. One incautious move, and you would have decided you were suffering a relapse and placed yourself in the care of the doctors again, out of reach."

A sudden savage joy filled Colin's mind. He exploded. "You mean I never was really insane?"

"No more than was due to the shock of being parted from your beloved Esther. At worst that might be termed depression. The rest"—Kolok shrugged—"was due to contact from over here."

"Oh, that's wonderful!" Colin exclaimed. "I was so frightened . . . Go on, for pity's sake!"

"Accordingly Telthis adopted an indirect approach. Hints to a believer in the Real Truth who works for your firm ensured that you were sent to Melbourne. Simply to place you in the same city as Vanessa confirmed what Telthis had suspected. But on that side of Earth there were no temples of the Real Truth we could make contact through. In this world what you call Australia is a wilderness uninhabited by man. It was necessary to bring Vanessa to the northern hemisphere, preferably not to New York for fear that the forces released at your meeting might be too strong to control, but to London, where there is a long-established seat of the cult. Losing what you call the British Isles would be no great hardship in our world; they are chilly and misty, and serve us as no more than a kind of colossal plantation."

"Losing them!" Vanessa repeated. "What do you mean?"

Kolok shrugged. "Telthis reasoned that it might become necessary to destroy you, for instance by burying you beneath a mountain, which even he could not accomplish without certain—ah—incidental damage."

Vanessa stared for a long second, then gave a shaky little laugh. "I can believe that," she said. "So it was one of your Real Truth people who lured me to London?"

"Of course. Not knowing where to turn when you were stranded there, you were glad to accept help when it was offered by another member of the cult."

"Larry was *ordered* to befriend me?" The words were faint.

"Not only to befriend but to marry you." There was compassion in Kolok's tone. "Even after living with your husband, you can have no conception of the degree of obedience Telthis can already command across the barrier in your world."

It was now too dark to see the expression on Vanessa's face, but she clutched her purse as though she were strangling someone.

"But now he's brought us together," Colin said, "what does Telthis plan to do with us?"

"He is assembling his forces for the invasion of your world. Meantime, he will simply keep you here, with no food and with little water. When your resistance has been lowered it will be easier for the adepts to pick at your minds. In a week, or less, you will have forgotten that you ever hated him. You will be his willing accomplices in the conquest of Earth, and together you will open the way for the coming of the Perfect Man."

"The Real Truth," Vanessa said. "It's your universal religion on this side, isn't it? But—who is the Perfect Man?"

Kolok laughed without humor. "Telthis, of course!"

Eventually Colin said, "But can nothing be done to stop him?"

"I am here in the hope that we can hinder him. Whether hindrance will suffice . . ." Kolok shook his head.

"But even though he rules the world, it's a poor and primitive world compared to ours! I mean, it must be, if that court of his is the finest he can boast!"

"Ah, don't be misled. No weapon in your world is swift or

deadly enough to strike down even an apprentice adept, let alone Telthis."

"We have computers that react infinitely faster than a man can think!"

"But have you one which can turn backward in time to an earlier moment, revise its own decisions of a second before?" Kolok uttered a sour chuckle. "No, believe me, mere speed is of no avail against a skilled adept of the Real Truth. Telthis could halt an aircraft in flight as surely as a stone wall, explode a shell before it left the muzzle of a gun, or trigger a nuclear bomb while it still lay in its arsenal. And if resistance is offered to him, he will do that!"

"But you are resisting him," Vanessa said. "Who are you?"

A shadow crossed Kolok's face. "The first man of my world, in ten thousand years, to have a vision of another way of life. The first to be shown that society need not consist of an elite of adepts and a horde of slaves. Though I was the first to step across the barrier, though I was as eager as Telthis himself at the beginning, it was because I'd never conceived of a life where naked power was not the only criterion of a man's worth. Doubtless to you your world has many faults; to me who have known only the rule of Telthis and his predecessor, it seemed like paradise."

"Have other adepts crossed over? Have they not come to the same conclusion?"

"Perhaps they might have done but that Telthis became alerted. I think I alone—and one other whom you will meet —can close our minds against total control. I do not believe that I could destroy Telthis if he challenged me, but I'm sure I could weaken him. Therefore he has avoided a confrontation. To be weak, for someone in his position, is to be deposed and probably dead."

His manner changed a little, and his tone grew almost conversational. "We have reached this point quicker than I dared hope. I feared you might not be open to conviction since the powers we wield in our world are always dismissed as superstition in yours. Time enough remains before I make my bid to get you away for another few questions to be asked and answered. What do you most want to be told?"

"You said you're going to help us escape?" Colin snapped. "Back to—to our own side?"

"That I cannot guarantee. But it's worth gambling that your disappearance will severely delay his plans. If I win another breathing space, I may be able to strike at him so hard that he has to abandon his dream of invasion. I have conceived a plan . . . But I should not even speak of it. It's still a dream."

"What about Larry?" Vanessa said suddenly. "He always talks as though he's a sort of member of the inner circle of the Real Truth cult. Has he any—well—powers?"

"None at all. He's a tool. He was recruited solely to ensure that the staging of Real Truth rituals was impressive in terms that would appeal to people in your world. Telthis cares no more for his cat's paws than for the man he burned alive to impress you."

"I should have guessed," Vanessa muttered, her voice as cold as winter wind.

Colin waited; when she added nothing more, he said, "The black shadow things, like what I used to see when I thought I was insane. I know now that they're real—this side of the barrier, at any rate—because they were used to bind us when we were taken before Telthis. But what are they?"

"In your terms they are difficult to describe. As I told you, they are called *trnak*." Kolok pondered for a moment. "It is possible for an adept to . . . stop himself. Your science would regard it as the generation of a field which inhibits entropy. The process is nonreversible, so only someone contemplating suicide would try it deliberately. But one can be forced to undertake it."

"You have so many adepts you can waste them on things like tying up a couple of helpless intruders?"

"The power gene is widespread now in our world. Would you not expect it to be, given that the elite can take their pick of women among the commoners? But its use is jealously guarded. Sometimes a commoner child is allowed to join the ranks of the adepts, though very seldom; there is an apprentices' school here in Egla-Garthon, but its enrollment never exceeds a hundred pupils. For the less fortunate children who display signs of the power, as for idiots and morons and those trainee adepts who have offended Telthis, the penalty is to be compelled to enter stasis. Once the field is returned to its source by command of a senior adept, he or she is forever more still than stone. Each *trnak* has indeed cost a human life —if not already, then soon."

"The Medusa!" Vanessa exclaimed.

"Perhaps," Kolok said with a shrug. "I sometimes wonder how much of what you regard as legend is due to a faint recollection of a time when we had not drifted so far apart. We have no objective history, you know; our memories have passed directly from mind to mind, and now and then the sto-

139

ry has been altered by a self-glorifying tyrant. Of course his successors usually tried to correct his lies, but doubtless they lied in their turn, also. . . ." He seemed to be listening to some sound that Colin and Vanessa could not catch and now rose smoothly to his feet.

"Time is running out. Come with me."

There was a thud from outside, and the door swung open. In the flickering light of a torch the guard could be seen slumped unconscious on a wooden stool; the thud had been the noise of his club falling. No one else was in sight. But of course that meant little.

In this world people might be watching without using their eyes.

X

They emerged safely from torch-lit passages at the head of a stairway leading down toward a courtyard open to the night sky. Kolok, halting, pointed, and there was movement below: An ox took a pace forward, and a crude farm cart whose after-part was screened with thick cloth rolled protestingly over the flags.

"It isn't a pretty vehicle," he muttered. "But it's the best I can do. Adepts have no need to worry about transportation, and commoners are forbidden anything less basic than carts. Were I to use mental force, though, it would alert every adept between here and Algnu-Bastharn, half around the world."

"Where are you sending us?" Colin whispered.

"To a place where I think Telthis's searchers will fail to locate you. When I have made certain they're on a false track, I'll rejoin you."

"Will the trip take long?"

"You'll be there by the middle of the fifth watch. We count time here by the sun, ten watches to a night and ten to a day. In your terms, half an hour before midnight. Roughly an hour from now." He cocked his head.

"You'd best get going. Things are about to happen here, and I can't make out what kind of things. Ah—good luck! In your world that means something. Everything in mine is at the mercy of one man's whims! But in the hope that that will change, I say again—*good luck!*"

He faded into the passage from which they had come. Colin and Vanessa hastened down the stairs and scrambled on to the rear of the cart, drawing the cover over them; it was made of a canvaslike fabric, stiff and thick. There was a strong animal smell. They caught only a glimpse of the driver, who kept his head stolidly to the front. Whether he knew what he was doing, whether he was blindly obeying Kolok's orders because they came from a senior adept, or whether Kolok had taken control of his mind as Telthis had done with the old crone of an interpreter, they could not guess and were disinclined to wonder.

As soon as their weight tilted the clumsy vehicle, the ox leaned on the traces, and the wheels turned; creak-grind, creak-grind, the axles kept up a monotonous objection.

Colin put his arm around Vanessa. Now night had fallen, the air was not just cool but positively cold, as though the weather-controlling adepts Kolok had mentioned had overdone it a little. He said, hoping to lighten her mood, "This is a hell of a way to travel, isn't it?"

"Logical, isn't it?" she countered. "If the adepts here can travel everywhere by an act of will, they probably watch out for any sign of inventiveness among the commoners and clamp right down on anyone who's fool enough to try and design a machine."

"Hmm!" Struck by a sudden thought, Colin produced his flashlight and thumbed the switch, confirming that it still didn't work. "Yes, that figures. Remember how your watch quit for good?"

"After we were brought over to this side for the first time, back in Tippet Lane," she said with a nod. "Yes, if this is a world where machines are forbidden . . . Wait a moment, though. Your watch started going again, didn't it?"

"Yes, but yours was electric. Mine's a regular spring-wound type. Processes as basic as that—or the friction which causes a match to light—can't be interfered with. Anything more advanced, though, is probably damped down by the massed subconscious of the adept elite." He tucked the flashlight back in his pocket, frowning. "Wish I'd thought of asking Kolok about that! But it does all hang together, doesn't it? Ox carts, clubs and swords, buildings of timber virtually unimproved for thousands of years . . . ! I'm sure I'm right. The adepts must have stopped anyone developing anything which might rival their natural powers. It's as though one of those *trnaks* has settled on the whole of human imagination!"

"As it was in the beginning, is now, and if Telthis has his way, ever shall be!" Vanessa muttered. "Excuse me if I sound blasphemous, but the Real Truthers seem to have set an example."

She added after a pause, "Colin, I'm sorry, but I can't keep up with you. You seem to be coping with this crazy world—I mean, here you are reasoning things out, fitting it all together. . . ."

"I'll tell you why," he said shortly. "It's because I thought I was crazy and might go crazy again, and all of a sudden I've found out that it wasn't true. Someone did it to me. And I'm going to get even with him if it's the last thing I do!"

"I . . ." She hesitated. "I think maybe I ought to say this even if it's not very kind. When we first met, you know, I wasn't terribly impressed with you. I think now it must have been because you were afraid of losing your mind again. It made you—I don't know—diffident, overcautious, too *detached!* Yes, that's what I'm getting at! When we first met in London, I was shaken to the bedrock of my mind by what happened to us, but you were inhumanly calm. Did you know that?"

"I can see it now," he answered. "And you're right. It must have been because I was fighting like hell against anything that might tip me back into insanity."

"I like you a lot better now," she said. "And I'm glad you're with me here. But . . . No, damn it, I can't keep up! I'm practically dropping! I know I ought to be concerned and excited and the rest of it, but what I most want to do is fall asleep. Do you mind?"

"Very sensible, given that Kolok won't be rejoining us for some while. I'd like to do the same, but I'm afraid I might have nightmares. . . . You go ahead, though, if you can."

She wriggled down on the floor of the wagon and stretched out in the least uncomfortable position she could find. Just before she relaxed, she caught at his hand and brushed it with her lips; he responded by stroking her sleek hair—and then she was instantly asleep. The moon was nearly full, and the sides of the wagon were punctuated with cracks almost wide enough to put a finger through. By the wan rays that seeped in, Colin could see her face, as composed as a child's.

The axles creaked continuously, and now and then they encountered a bump that demonstrated that even such an elementary luxury as cart springs made of rawhide had not been developed in this world. Colin shook his head in pure wonderment at the idea that he was crossing Manhattan in this crude cart covered with a canvas awning. How many other worlds might not lie beside the one he hailed from? If two had been riven apart by the chance mating of a brother with his sister, could not there be a million separate universes, or a billion?

Yet Kolok had referred specifically to *one* woman in whom the gene had cropped out. He had called it a mutation. Most mutations, Colin knew, were unfavorable; moreover, nature was prodigal with reproductive cells. Given that the greater part of human existence had been spent in primitive, precivilized conditions, he could well imagine that when a child appeared who displayed strange abilities, the commonest reaction would be: *Kill!* Had they not burned witches very recently, as the world's age went?

So there might not be a multiplicity of parallel worlds, after all, if Kolok was correct in saying that only the massed minds of mankind could alter the nature of reality.

It strained his already frail powers of credulity to believe that a child capable of overcoming terrified and determined adults could have been born very often in a savage tribe. No, the most probable conclusion was that any other world whose history had been changed in the same manner must have been so radically deflected from the—what to call it?—the "normal" path of human development as to be forever unreachable.

On the other hand, if the same thing happened in a civilized community, and the child, instead of being exterminated at once, were allowed to grow up and . . . ?

No, he was too tired to think that through to a conclusion. Also he was weak; he had not eaten since about noon, and he was sick with hunger because he had vomited when Telthis burned his slave alive. Best, if he could, to copy Vanessa's example and get some rest.

He leaned his cheek on her soft hair and shut his eyes, hoping at least that even if he could not sleep he might doze and refresh himself.

The cart jolted to a halt. The driver said nothing, but after a moment in which he blinked and tried frantically to remember where he was, Colin realized that this stage of their journey must be over. He woke Vanessa, and they clambered stiffly to the ground. They were on a rough, muddy track. On a distant hillside firelight shone through the ill-shuttered windows of a lowly cottage. Clouds had risen to veil the moon; the setting was eerie.

The driver prodded his ox with a vicious six-foot goad, and the ponderous wagon creaked away. They were alone.

"Do we just wait?" Vanessa whispered.

"I guess so." Colin shivered; up to now the covering on the wagon had protected them, but up here they were exposed to a chill breeze smelling of the sea. "Let's get out of the wind," he said, pointing to a stunted hedge paralleling the road.

There was no border to the road apart from that—nothing so wasteful of land as a grass verge, even. The agriculture here was doubtless as rudimentary as the architecture. Every available square yard was dug over. Beyond the hedge was a field of what he guessed might be turnips, or some similar root crop. Their leaves were scanty and ill doing.

"It's the poverty which terrifies me," Vanessa said. "That—that hovel over there, in the middle of what for us is New York! The capital city of the entire world can be only a couple of miles away, and . . . Oh, it's frightening!"

"Yes!" Colin shuddered.

"And did you see the faces of the people in the temple?"

"Yes, they were nauseating. Not so much in the front rows —I suppose they let the better-off commoners sit up there— but at the back, where they were even shabbier and dirtier. It made me think of what you said about the people turning up for the service in New York. I couldn't see it then, but over on this side you simply can't mistake it."

"Right! Pinched and fatuously eager, the way I suppose the Chinese must have been in the bad old days, starving themselves to buy opium because it was their only escape from unbearable reality."

"And that's what they hope to do to our world, with the help of their Real Truth dupes," Colin muttered. "Vanessa, you must have met several of Larry's friends in the cult. Do you think any of them came from this side?"

She shook her head. "Didn't Kolok say that only master adepts can make the trip? And if he's right in saying that Larry is no more than a convenient tool, you wouldn't expect people like that to waste time in his company."

"Yet we were able to *walk* through the barrier! Accidentally!" Colin thought of that sensation of falling an infinite distance between one step and the next.

"That must be because of what Kolok mentioned: When we

come together, we channel some kind of force which— Oh, Colin, *look!*"

She clutched his arm and pointed across the field toward the soft blur of light that was the moon filtered by high clouds. Something crooked and angular was glimmering there, approaching them swiftly, several feet above the ground. It was far too big for a bird. Did they have alien creatures in this alien world?

It swooped toward the road and came to a hovering halt a few paces from where they were standing. In the wan light it looked ghastly, a vague and awful specter, and then suddenly it spoke in a pleasant treble voice and told them not to be afraid.

Instantly they realized: Flying was a human ability here, and this weird apparition was no more than a talented child.

"Who are you?" Colin demanded.

"I am called Ishimu, so please you," said the child in an accent like Welsh but more heavily inflected. "I am an apprentice of the temple in Egla-Garthon, and I am sent by Master Kolok to guide you to shelter. I regret I am not here before."

Colin was beginning to make the boy out more clearly now. He stood about ten feet away. He was very thin, with an overlarge head and arms like sticks, and wore only a loose, short gown open in front despite the chill of the night air. And then the clouds left the moon for an instant, and Vanessa gasped.

Ishimu was *not* standing. He was poised in midair, a yard above the road. He could not have stood—perhaps had never stood—for his legs were bent up like warped matches under his hips. Also, his eyes were closed, and somehow they both knew by intuition that it made no difference whether they were open or shut.

There was a wealth of sadness in the tone with which he commented on their reaction. "You are surprised. Do you not have people such as me in your world? Master Kolok has told me that your world is better than ours."

Embarrassed, Colin said, "Yes, we—we do have people like you, Ishimu. We were just a little startled, that's all."

"But you do not find them at every street corner," said Ishimu bitterly. "Master Kolok told me. You do not see in every town children less fortunate than even I, less able to make their minds serve instead of feet, who are crippled as I was by a hungry mother to excite pity and beg bread!"

"In India . . ." Vanessa's voice quavered. "I think they used to do it there."

"They *do* do it here," said Ishimu. "But let us waste no

more time. I am to take you to a place of concealment until Master Kolok arrives. Prepare yourselves, for I gather this is new to you."

The pressure of weight on Colin's soles ceased abruptly, and with Vanessa beside him, he found himself standing a yard above the road. Ishimu had floated up level with them.

Panic gripped him for an instant. The thought of being wafted through the air by a boy who could be no more than ten years old frightened him so much that his mind rebelled, and he dropped six inches.

"If you remain calm," said Ishimu dispassionately, "you will be quite safe. We go now."

Colin took a deep breath, ordering himself to relax. At once they were streaming upward and away; the ruddy glow of the nearby cottage's window passed beneath and was gone. He found he was close enough to Vanessa to take her hand and squeezed it in a wordless attempt to convey his pure delight in this experience. It was dreamlike to soar through the night in total silence with no effort.

And the view was fantastic! It was awe-inspiring to see this countryside bare of buildings apart from the occasional hut or shanty. The East River glimmered, innocent of bridges; he glimpsed a bulky dark shape by a track at the water's edge that might have been the boathouse for a ferry. If he strained his eyes, he could just make out the Palisades.

Marvelous! Magnificent! This ability to fly like the birds!

But the same power, he reflected more soberly a moment later, had called forth Telthis.

And is that a fair bargain?

XI

And then they drifted down, feather-light, to a clearing in a copse. Smoke from the chimney of a wooden hut stung their eyes as they passed briefly through it. Its door swung wide, and the boy said, "Enter! I have prepared everything against your arrival."

"You came from here to meet us?" Vanessa hazarded.

"By no means." Ishimu sounded mildly surprised. "I have never been here before. The print of my awareness on this place might have led the men of Telthis— Ah, but that of course would mean nothing to you. You must inquire of Master Kolok for more details of the reason."

Silently they entered the hut. It had only this one room. The windows were shuttered, and drafts through chinks around their edges made fat candles gutter in wall-mounted sconces. But the dirt floor was strewn with clean beach sand, and there were pleasant scents in the air. On a hearth apparently made of some sort of pottery and under a smokehood of the same substance leading to the chimney, a fire of large logs was burning; above it, on a spit, a joint of meat turned slowly, shedding an occasional droplet of fat into the flames. Rough-hewn wooden chairs surrounded a trestle table in the center of the room, and a wooden bed spread with sheepskins occupied the length of the wall opposite the door.

"Be seated," Ishimu invited. "You hunger? You thirst?"

The chairs grated back of their own accord. Slices of meat parted from the roasting joint; platters floated from a shelf, accepted the meat, and settled to the table. Two mugs likewise drifted down, and a jug of spring water, and some cakes of gritty dark bread.

No longer astonished, Colin nonetheless wondered at the absence of any hint of strain on Ishimu's face while he was performing these feats of telekinesis. Could it be that this boy was the "one other" Kolok had spoken of who might be capable of withstanding Telthis? Certainly his powers must be incredible if he could carry two adults miles through the air and make ready this hut for their arrival without ever approaching it!

"You will pardon me," Ishimu said, crossing the room to lower his shriveled haunches on the piled sheepskins. "I must ascertain what Master Kolok is doing and when he will be here."

He bent his head, folded his hands in his lap, and became totally immobile.

"Let's make the most of our chance and eat something," Colin muttered to Vanessa. She nodded and set to.

There was no cutlery, nor other food than the meat and the coarse nubbly bread, but they both ate voraciously and emptied the jug of water. At last, with a sigh of contentment, Colin leaned back and offered cigarettes, lighting them with a long splinter from the fire. In the same moment Ishimu stirred and spoke quietly.

"There is much confusion. I can make out little except that Master Kolok will not have reached here one watch from now. I shall try again later. Meanwhile I sense that you are weary. Make use of this bed if you like." He floated away from it and took the vacant chair.

His brief doze in the cart had satisfied Colin for the time being, but Vanessa accepted promptly, lay down, and went to sleep almost at once.

Shuffling his chair closer to the fire, as much for the sake of its light as its warmth—the candles were of little help—Colin looked frankly at Ishimu and voiced a question that had been haunting him while he ate.

"Ishimu, you have so many powers. Can't you . . . ?"

"What?"

"Well—heal your disability."

The cripple laughed as harshly as his unbroken voice would allow. "There are limits to all talents, Master Hooper! And is it not as well? The only consolation to those whom Telthis grinds down is that with age his powers must fail, or perhaps some pestilence will strike him. Not, indeed, that one could expect his successor to be less cruel. It is the way of our world. But, as to what you were saying . . . !"

His tone altered, and he turned his sightless gaze on Colin with a hint of eagerness. "Master Kolok has told me that in your world men are not so prone to sickness. Is it truly possible to fight disease and mend the breaking of the body?"

"Sometimes," Colin said slowly. "Tell me, do you know about germs, the little creatures which infest the bloodstream of a sick person?"

Ishimu looked blank.

"Do you know that matter is made up of millions upon millions of little particles called atoms? Do you know that the stars are suns like the sun, but many times farther away?"

"This is true?" demanded Ishimu incredulously, and Colin sighed. His ignorance was logical. Here, they relied on their senses. To a man's unaided perception solid is solid and a star is a light nailed on the sky. Germs and atoms must be as undetectable to Ishimu's mind as to his own naked eye.

Small wonder they had stagnated so long!

"Tell me about this world of yours," said Ishimu with a touch of envy. "I have learned of it from Master Kolok—enough to know that it's a strange and wonderful place—but he has never had time to answer all my questions."

So Colin told him. A little. Not varnishing the facts, not concealing the sad truth that his world, too, was acquainted with cruelty and greed, with war and poverty and crime, yet the effect was as if he had been telling a fairy tale. Incredulity struggled in Ishimu's face with desperate longing to believe that such marvels could be real.

"Oh, how is it that you have achieved so much?" he cried at last.

Colin hesitated. "Perhaps," he said thoughtfully, "it's because in my world man had to work in ways your ancestors had no need of. He used his hands and his intelligence and figured things out. Here, everything seems to have come too easily. Savages with infinite power had no reason to restrain their animal instincts. What they wanted, they took; what they couldn't have, they broke like jealous children. Am I right, Ishimu? Tell me about your world."

"I can do better," Ishimu said, a little pride entering his voice. "I can show it to you."

He felt in a pouch on the girdle that held his robe together and produced a mirror of polished metal no larger than his palm. Deftly he held it up to Colin's face so that the flame of the nearest candle was reflected in it, then set to twisting it in a repeated spiral. The bright light flickered to the center, vanished, reappeared at the edge, spun inward again. Colin felt a spasm of alarm at recognizing the same rhythm as was kept by the hypnotic white discs in the temples of the Real Truth; then he relaxed, realizing he had nothing to fear from Ishimu.

His mind expanded, and he *saw*.

Afterward, he wondered whether it had been a mere illusion, or whether in some supernormal fashion Ishimu had transferred real, present-time images into his awareness. However it was achieved, the impact was vivid—and terrifying.

He saw a line of commoners, cold, hungry, half-naked, waiting at the gate of a temple for the daily service, waiting to be told that all their suffering was worthwhile because it had been decreed by the Perfect Man. He saw peasant farmers struggling to wrest a living from their overused land, scratching it with wooden ploughs drawn by bony oxen, or with no help at all except their own weak muscles and their wives'. He saw soldiers patrolling unpaved streets in leather jerkins, their clubs on their shoulders, pouncing on the crippled beggars who were marginally less prosperous than they and stealing even the crusts dropped in their begging bowls . . . That had an aura of greater authenticity than some of the other scenes; perhaps it was based on Ishimu's own experience.

Scenes of misery gave place to a vision of luxury. In a sandy, hot country that he thought might correspond to the Egypt of his own world, fine white houses belonging to adepts basked under a steel-blue sky, just out of earshot of the cries from the fruit groves, the bucket pumps, the threshing floors where slaves were being whipped to work, which the mind of one of their masters could have disposed of in a minute. Again, on an island where luxuriant palms and gorgeous flowers abounded, there was a palace with hundreds upon hundreds of rooms, lavishly decorated, tiled with marble, jasper, and mother-of-pearl . . . and all empty, awaiting the whim that might bring Telthis here to escape the northern winter, while slaves were packed head to foot on beds like racks in a foul-smelling barracks beyond the hill.

Slowly the picture of the world grew to completion. In every corner of the planet where the adepts held sway—which meant on four continents, only Australia having failed to tempt them—the commoners lived and died, perhaps without traveling more than a day's walk from home in their entire lifetime. They regarded it as good fortune to be enslaved into an adept's retinue, and small wonder, for their "freedom" was so drab. Draft animals pulled what vehicles they boasted: camels here, llamas there, horses (but very rarely) in another place, and for the most part oxen. A few fishing communities owned boats; a few trading rafts plied the larger rivers, hauled upstream by oxen or by gangs of men in chains, allowed to drift back with the current. But there were no ships. When the adepts could cross oceans by an act of will, what need of them? Better to exploit the sea as a natural prison wall, shut in the bodies as well as the minds of the common people!

And everywhere there spied and probed the viceroys of Telthis. However jealous they might be of his supreme power, it was in their interest as well as his to stamp out any hint of originality, for originality might lead to rebellion.

This must not happen to my world! Colin thought.

Yet if even Kolok doubted that he could prevent Telthis from achieving his goal, what could be done by an ordinary man with no supernormal talents?

The pictures in his mind faded. With the taste of despair in his mouth, he opened his eyes to find Kolok in his splendid robe standing beside the table.

XII

The adept looked weary and impatient. He spoke to Ishimu in his own tongue; the few brief words were supplemented by rapid changes of expression and several gestures. Colin deduced that much more was passing than the content of the spoken utterance.

Ishimu floated off his chair, made a leave-taking sign to Colin not unlike the Indian *namasthi*, and vanished through the open door faster than the eye could follow.

Disturbed, Vanessa sat up, rubbing her eyes.

"At least you've had the chance to eat and rest," Kolok muttered. "Oh, but I've never seen such a hornet's nest!" Overcome by fatigue, he sat down on the chair Ishimu had vacated.

"Where has Ishimu gone?" Vanessa asked.

"Back to the apprentices' dormitory in the Egla-Garthon temple."

"Under Telthis's very nose?" Colin said disbelievingly.

"Why not? He'll be safer there than anywhere else. You don't understand the nature of deceit in this world, my friend. It's far easier for him to convince a small number of key persons that he never left the city tonight than it would be to hide in the loneliest forest."

"Is he the 'one other' you mentioned who might stand against Telthis?"

"Yes." Kolok gazed into the fire. "No one knows but I the full extent of his powers. He is something unparalleled in either of our histories, that boy. Beside him, Telthis at that age was a bumbling incompetent. But he will never have the chance to prove his skill."

"What do you mean?" Vanessa demanded.

"We have looked to see. And in a little while he—stops."

"*Dies?*"

"Or loses his mind. He will burn out; his frame is too weak for the power it contains."

"Does he know?" Colin ventured.

"Yes, of course."

A shadow seemed to fall across them for a moment. Colin felt an irrational tightening in his throat.

But before he could speak again, Kolok was saying, "The delay in joining you is regretted, but your disappearance was discovered by Telthis himself, and he made an example of the guards who let you get away, requiring me and other adepts to be present. Fortunately it runs counter to his vanity to believe that someone he himself chose for so important a task as the first mission into your world could turn against him; so far he has shown no hint that he suspects what I'm doing. He thinks he dug a trap for himself by bringing you together, that you discovered your powers while in prison and released yourselves. Having found no trace of you in the city, he has alerted four continents. Adepts are feeling for signs of the fantastic but uncontrolled mental activity he presumes you to have developed, while patrols hunt for clues to your physical presence. Vainly, of course.

"What he will do next, I can't be sure. Someone with Telthis's power can generate a kind of mist around his future actions. So many possibilities are open to him. But what's most likely is that he will eventually go into trance himself, to make a personal check on the stories his viceroys relay to him from abroad, for fear that you have mastered one or more of them and compelled him to report falsely. If so, that will give us the chance to steal back into the city, and into the temple, and return by the tunnel under it to your own world."

"Is there no other way back?"

"I know of none. At that place the barrier has been weakened over months and years by the massed minds of the temple congregation. Even with your help it's the only crossing point I would attempt in my present exhausted condition."

"Speaking of help," Colin said, "is there no one but Ishimu you can trust over here?"

"No one at all. If you can ask that question, it's plain that even now you don't understand the situation here. Telthis's mastery is absolute, extending even to the minds of his subjects. Only I, of all the adepts in the world, have been able to refuse him access to my inmost thoughts. Compelled to recognize me as next to him in skill, he chose me, as I told you, to be first into your world. At worst he would lose a dangerous rival; at best he would gain fuller information in a shorter time than any other adept could obtain."

"Once you'd changed your mind about cooperating with Telthis," Colin ventured, "could you not have stayed on our side and used your powers to block the entry of anyone he sent after you? Is there a way of doing that?"

"There is," Kolok said after a pause. "Unfortunately I am not currently inclined to suicide."

"Suicide? Oh! The *trnak?*"

"Precisely. In fact, that's one thing that worries me at this moment—the possibility that, expecting your return to the tunnel, Telthis will close the weak point in the continuum with an inhibited-entropy field. The loss of one access point will be a nuisance to him, but no more than that. Another can be created eventually."

"Something puzzles me," Vanessa said. "In all the time I knew him"—Colin noticed but did not comment on her use of the past tense—"Larry never talked about these superpowers as though they really existed. He did say things now and then about what the Perfect Man would ultimately be able to do, but I'm not sure he took that part of it very seriously. If adepts from here have been sent across to our side, why did they not give demonstrations, which would have convinced people by millions, instead of recruiting an odd follower here and there?"

"Because, in his vanity, Telthis wishes to be revealed to your world with no forerunners. He has strictly ordered his agents never to use their powers while they are over there. I myself have had to abide by that rule; disobedience would have been fatal . . . Silence, please, for one moment!"

He raised a hand, and his face locked into a mask of concentration as complete as Telthis's when burning his slave. It lasted perhaps half a minute; then he relaxed and rose to his feet.

"Good! A mental sweep of this area has just been carried out, and the adept concerned perceived a convincing illusion of bare ground identical to what he would have seen yesterday and will see tomorrow. We can now return to Egla-Garthon, confident that the search has passed over us. Ishimu flew you here, didn't he? Then you will not be alarmed by *this*."

The candles on the walls went out; the fire died into smoking embers. Bed, table, chairs, all seemed to break apart and crumble dustily. Last of all the hut's walls dissolved, and they stood under the sky.

"That, too, is one of Telthis's weapons," said Kolok glacially. "I think it not, and it is not."

The weight came off their feet, and suddenly they were flying toward the city at such a pace, tears almost blinded their windswept eyes.

The pattern of Egla-Garthon was simple. Its main roads—tracks, rather—led, like the radial strands of a cobweb, toward a complex of tall buildings in the center: the temple, the palace, an army barracks, and warehouses for the taxes in kind that the commoners had to pay to support Telthis's household. Farther out, there were a few modest but substantial houses belonging to merchants, jewelers, armorers, and other artificers and traders in favor at court; then once more a scattering of tall buildings, the homes of adepts, and last a fringe of sad hovels forming the outskirts.

Here and there a torch carried head high bespoke a patrol or a wealthy nonadept being borne in a litter on the way to visit a friend, but those sparks were the only sign of life. Colin felt a mounting sense of futility. The entire world, he now knew, was like this city, held in a hammerlock by the effortless power of a few men whose dreams turned to reality at a thought.

There was a sudden cry from Kolok, who hitherto had been speaking in a quiet tone, explaining what could be seen below. At the same time they felt a vast pressure on their minds.

"They've spotted us! They're thinking me down, and I can't hold you!"

The buildings rushed to meet them. As they fell, there were shouts: Doors and windows were flung wide; men with torches crowded into the open. Even if they survived this headlong plunge, what chance would they have of escaping pursuit in that maze of poky alleys when half the population had been alerted?

Against his will, Colin cried out. They were so low he could see the highlights on the cobbles where the moon washed the street. In one more second—!

They checked abruptly. The shock made him feel as though his guts were tearing loose. The world spun and blurred and dizzied him. When his sight cleared, they were all standing huddled in a dark alcove, a stone wall hard at their backs.

"Saved!" Kolok muttered prayerfully.

"What did you do?" Vanessa demanded, half-staggering, having to clutch at Colin to keep her balance.

"I? Nothing. They were too strong for me. Ishimu must have come to our rescue. Never have I felt such a blast of power! I swear, there were twenty adepts or more driving us down." He shivered. "Here, though, we are safe for the moment."

"Where are we?"

"Between the temple and the palace. Telthis has always feared that some rival might take command of the minds of the congregation, the world's largest, and launch an attack on him during a service. So he has screened the intervening space with *trnak* fields. But at best we have won a respite. Though the *trnak* stasis prevents a direct onslaught, there remains one weapon we are not protected from. Look, they are deploying it already."

He pointed down the cul-de-sac in which they stood. At its mouth, shadows a little too black melted and reformed shiftingly, menacingly.

"It will take a little while," Kolok said. "But a diffuse *trnak* field can always be reinforced." He added after a second: "In this world, it is a matter of honor to meet death with dignity. I will lend you what calmness I can."

To Colin this seemed like far too meek a surrender. He burst out, "But if we're so close to the temple, doesn't that mean we're also close to the tunnel? You said the barrier was weakest in this area!"

"And so it is, but the stasis hampers my mind, as though I were clad in sheets of lead!" Kolok thrust his hands toward the stars, close together like those of a man trapped by gyves, before letting them fall back to his sides.

No! Colin raged silently. *It mustn't end like this!*

Still as a sculpture now, Kolok was preparing to meet his doom with honorable dignity. The hell with that! It was too much to ask him to die without telling the brutal despot of this world what he thought of him!

He took two fierce strides toward the gathering *trnak*. "Telthis!" he bellowed. "Can you hear me? I know you're there— you must be there! Did you think you could scare us with your sadistic tricks? Did you think we'd give in and tamely work for you because you're bound to win? Well, I say to *hell* with you and all your fawning dupes! We aren't downtrodden slaves where I come from—we haven't been broken by you and the likes of you over ten thousand years! We don't have a million slaves to every free man! You can see across the world, you can build and destroy and fly through the air, and you think that makes you special! Well, in my world *anyone* can fly who wants to, *anyone* can see and hear across an ocean, and—heaven help us—nowadays one man can lay a city low! But we had to learn how to do that! We had to rack our brains and blister our hands and in the end we made it happen! Do you still imagine you can grind us down? Do you think you can stamp on three billion people and leave the print of your heel on all our faces? We'll see you in hellfire first!"

Yes, somehow a way would be found to stop Telthis. For otherwise the human race would have shown that it was unfit to live.

During his tirade the *trnak* had hesitated. Now they surged forward again, drifting slow as fog. The first had almost reached Colin when he found himself unable to wait passively for it any longer. A blaze of rage welled up in his mind, and he cursed it and the power behind it to the blackest pit he knew. He closed his eyes, and clenched his fists, and simply stood there, *hating* it.

"Colin! Colin!"

Vanessa's voice. *What—?*

And noise. And, when he blinked, bright lights. Faint in memory, mistaken for the impact of the *trnak,* the sensation of falling into an infinite abyss. Kolok and Vanessa were standing before him, staring at him with something akin to awe. Overhead, around, luckily screening them from late-night passersby, the sad dusty trees of . . .

"We're in Mann Square," Colin said incredulously. "My God. We're in New York."

XIII

"Ishimu?" Colin said from a dry throat. "Did he save us a second time?"

Kolok was regarding him in wonder. "Not Ishimu nor I nor Telthis himself could have opened the way in the grip of *trnak,*" he said. "How could I have been so blind? How could I not have known?"

He slammed fist into palm in a gesture of self-directed scorn.

"Known? Known what?"

"That Telthis was wrong!" Kolok exploded. "You do have the power—you must have it, though you've never learned to use it! And Telthis believed it would only appear in your children. There is still hope, do you understand? There is still hope of defeating him if I can instruct you in time—"

Colin put up his hands as though to ward off the flow of words. "No!" he said harshly. "No, after what I've seen in your world, I don't want the power! It's too much for anyone to be trusted with!"

"But if the only chance of stopping Telthis is to—" Kolok began. Vanessa interrupted.

"For heaven's sake, don't stand here arguing! The Real Truth headquarters is just across the road, and I'm so afraid somebody will recognize us!"

"Damned right," Colin agreed. "But we'd better not just walk away, not with Kolok in that robe. Look, you two stay here while I go find a cab!"

He hastened out of the concealment of the dusty trees and headed for the corner of the square farthest from the Real Truth temple.

And there was not an empty cab to be had. Fully five minutes' waving and shouting ended in complete failure. He grew more and more nervous and finally concluded that even though Kolok's robe would draw everyone's attention, it would be best to get away from this neighborhood as quickly as possible. Furious, he hurried back to where he had left his companions.

But the spot where they had been standing was vacant.

Thinking they must have drawn back into greater concealment among the trees, he peered about him and called out. The answer he received was not a welcome one.

"Don't move, Mr. Hooper," said a soft, hateful voice. "This weapon may not be comparable to those I gather they employ *elsewhere*, but it's perfectly adequate for its purpose."

He whirled. Emerging into plain view from behind a thick clump of shrubs, fair hair a little tousled but otherwise impeccably elegant, and with a smug expression of triumph on his face: Larry Adderley, holding a small automatic as though he well knew how to use it.

Sickly, Colin obeyed. A second figure appeared in Larry's wake. Even wearing conventional American clothing, there was no mistaking the fat adept he had overpowered beneath the Egla-Garthon temple. He prodded Colin's chest, waist, and crotch for concealed weapons—still, Colin realized, complying with Telthis's order not to use his supernormal powers over here for fear of stealing the thunder of the Perfect Man.

He stepped back with a satisfied grunt. Larry gestured with the gun before slipping it into the side pocket of his jacket.

"Remember I have this gun trained on you, Hooper. Walk slowly, please, toward the Seat of the Real Truth. No doubt you wish to rejoin your companions as quickly as possible, and that is where they have been taken."

This time Telthis's agents were making doubly sure. In a small, harshly lit room above the temple hall he found Vanessa and Kolok securely lashed to solid wooden chairs. Behind each of them stood a tall, heavyset man by way of guard. They might have belonged to Telthis's army or could as well have been hired on this side; they had the indefinable air of professional thugs. Also present was a third man whose hair was cut in the same curious fashion as Kolok's: another visiting adept. To Colin he seemed strangely familiar.

With a shove in the small of his back, Larry sent Colin stumbling across the floor. The adept looked him over and gave his captors a curt nod.

"Excellent, Adderley. You were admirably quick about it."

With a touch of petulance, Larry countered, "Thank you—but I understood I was entitled to be addressed as 'Master'!"

"If it makes you happy," the adept grunted, not according him so much as another glance. His eyes were fixed on Colin. "You seem to recognize me," he continued.

"It was you in Tippet Lane," Colin said slowly. "I remember your voice, though I hardly had a glimpse of your face."

Kolok spoke up in a defiant tone. "His name is Yovan, and in our language that means—"

"Shut up," Yovan said, and the nearer of the two goons dealt Kolok a casual blow across the mouth. He groaned, and a dribble of blood oozed down his chin. Colin was horrified. Now that he was known to be working against Telthis, why did Kolok not use his powers? There was no more to be lost and much might be gained . . . But perhaps he was still too exhausted. The strain of being forced to the ground by the massed minds of over twenty adepts could well have taken a long-lasting toll.

In any case, there was no time to reason it out. Colin felt himself seized by both the thugs, and despite his best efforts he, too, was forced down on a chair, to which Larry lashed him with strong, new rope, chuckling faintly.

When he was secure, the fat man said something to Yovan in his own tongue and received a nod of assent. From a wall shelf he brought a large pottery jar and three shallow cups, which Yovan filled with a dark, pungent-smelling liquid.

"You will drink this," he said. "After that we shall have no more trouble from you."

"What is it?" Vanessa whispered.

Kolok, recovered a little from the blow on his face, said, "A decoction of a plant I don't know your name for. A soporific.

They intend to put us into coma. Or kill us, maybe; it's fatal above a threshold dose."

"Oh, you're not going to enjoy a quick death," Larry said with relish. "Least of all you, Kolok, who turned on your master and betrayed him! We only plan to keep you quiet until tomorrow."

The two adepts exchanged scowling glances, as though they did not approve of the freedom of Larry's tongue.

"Tomorrow?" Colin said.

"Why, yes." Larry seemed to preen. "As my—ah—beloved wife has probably informed you, I'm here to supervise a mass rally of believers in the Real Truth. It's a great honor, far greater than I ever expected, in fact." A rather nauseating look of adoration crossed his features.

"At this rally, which I conceived and will direct, the Perfect Man is to enter his new domain!"

"And you," Vanessa said clearly, "are looking forward to groveling in front of him, aren't you?"

Larry took two quick strides and confronted her, hand raised as though to smack her cheek. In midmovement he checked.

"No, you're not going to trap me like that," he said. "That's what you want, isn't it? You want to make me lose my temper and betray the Perfect Man, always in control, never swayed by ungovernable emotion."

So that was the image Telthis's agents were presenting to the followers of the Real Truth! Their dupes were in for a shock, Colin thought.

"The logical thing to do is quiet you," Larry went on. "And it would be poetically just for me to give you your draft myself. Master Yovan, by your leave!" He seized one of the waiting cups.

"If it amuses you, *Master* Adderley," Yovan said with thin contempt. Larry flushed, but ignored the gibe and set the cup to Vanessa's mouth, drawing back her hair with the other hand so that he could spill the liquid between her teeth.

"There," he said. "Poetic justice—*whaaa!*"

Vanessa had not been able to prevent the drug running into her mouth, but she had avoided swallowing it, and the moment he released her hair she had spat the whole revolting mouthful straight into his eyes.

Moaning, clawing at his face, Larry stumbled backward and crashed into the table on which the other cups stood, sending them flying. The fat adept gasped, but Yovan remained as still as stone.

"If you have quite finished, *Master* Adderley?" he said in a silky voice.

"My eyes! The bitch has blinded me!" Larry wailed.

"Swayed by ungovernable emotion!" Colin mocked. It was a petty insult, but the only weapon left to him, and he did not expect to wield it very much longer.

Larry groped his way to the door and staggered out, shouting for water. When he had gone, the fat adept shrugged, gathered up the shards of broken pottery, and also went out, presumably to refill the jar of drug.

So Vanessa had gained them a stay of execution. But what use could they make of it? Colin gazed anxiously at Kolok, and as though the latter had divined the question he wanted to put, was answered with a sad headshake.

There was no need to add words to know that his guess about Kolok's total exhaustion was correct. His heart sank. Still, perhaps there was a chance to plant a few seeds of discord.

"Due for a rude awakening, your Larry!" he said loudly to Vanessa. "When he actually meets Telthis, I mean!"

"Don't call him *mine*," Vanessa snapped.

"Kolok, what will Telthis do to him? Burn him alive, like the slave he killed just to impress us?" Out of the corner of his eye Colin was looking for a reaction on the part of the two guards, but none came.

"Like any invader, he's going to get rid of the people who helped him the most," he went on. "I wonder where these two big guys will be tomorrow—dead or in chains?"

Yovan, with a look between a smile and a sneer, said, "It's ingenious of you to try and worry these men. But you waste your breath. Both are as deaf as the walls."

"But—!" Colin began.

"You're thinking that they obey orders very smartly? So they do. They are trained to follow my signals." Yovan raised a hand meaningly. "Shall I instruct them to silence you? One well-placed blow, and a throat can become too painful to use for speaking."

Colin slumped against his bonds. With a glance full of sympathy Kolok said, "Oh, this Yovan will sing another tune one day, and pretty soon, at that. If I achieved nothing else, I have delayed Telthis's plans. His rule won't last more than ten years, and those like Yovan who have served him loyally will be the first to be crushed as would-be successors squabble for his throne."

"Only ten years?" Vanessa said. "But—but he isn't old."

"Not in your world. In mine, a man who reaches sixty is unusual, and by fifty an adept is growing weak. Someone with as many jealous rivals as Telthis . . ." He shrugged.

"You forget something," interrupted Yovan. "He is not staying in our world. He is coming to this one, with all its doctors and advanced medicine. I foresee that Telthis will enjoy at least twenty years more of excellent health, and by then we shall have taught all the billions of people over here the consequences of disobeying their supreme master. I made the better choice, Kolok, and you well know it!"

The fat adept reappeared in the doorway, and Yovan concluded, "Ah, here comes my colleague. Let us cut short this pointless chatter and consign you to a night's sound sleep!"

XIV

The crowd surged like a sea. Colin, dragged with Vanessa and Kolok to witness the end of their world, stared in sick dismay at the milling thousands who packed Washington Square. The alien drug was powerful; they had all three slumbered like logs in the room above the meeting hall until a few minutes ago when they had been brutally shaken awake and forced, stumbling at every other step, down to the street, into a car, and brought the few blocks north to the back of the Washington Square arch. Eager Real Truth dupes had taken them in charge, and now they were seated high on a portable platform erected around the arch to dominate the square.

The simple fact that the cult could take the whole square over for their rally implied that even before the advent of Telthis they were enjoying influence many older-established groups might envy.

If I dived off the platform head-first, maybe I could break my neck, Colin thought. *If it's true that Vanessa and I make it easier to come across from the other world, killing myself might . . .*

But the idea was foggy and remote. Some after-effect of the

drug muted all his reactions, as had the therapy during his nervous breakdown, and he lacked the energy even to rise to his feet.

And if he had been so dreadfully affected, doubtless Kolok must have suffered similarly. There was no hope of his making use of his supernormal talent at the moment; one could read his despair from the slack muscles of his face, the slumped attitude he had adopted in his chair.

How many of these people were Real Truthers hoping to witness their millennium? How many were local strollers, dismissing the rally as a sign of just another Village nut cult? How many were innocent folkniks, regarding Labor Day as an excuse to have two Sundays in this week, hunting some quiet spot where they could pick their instruments and sing? How many were tourists in the big city enthusiastically snapping pictures to show to their friends back home? There was no way of telling. The only certain fact was that the crowd was enormous—larger than the police had bargained for, to judge by the squad cars rolling up, the roaring motorcycle patrolmen, the occasional dehumanized crackle of a loud radio voice from the other side of the arch.

Correction: Add to that a second certainty. Everyone—conniving at the sell-out or totally ignorant—was due for the biggest shock of a lifetime.

It was almost time for the rally to begin. The police were forcing people back to make a clear path to the platform. Eyes squinting against the sun, the watchers allowed themselves to be herded while they tried to read the banners draped around the arch. They bore slogans culled from the precepts of the Real Truth, such as: *KNOWLEDGE* MOVES MOUNTAINS and YOUR MIND IS THE GREATEST THING IN THE WORLD and THE TRUTH MUST PREVAIL and MAN IS THE MEASURE AND THE MASTER.

Distant, solemn music could be heard. An air of expectancy settled on the crowd. Heads turned. Parents lifted children high for a better view.

Reluctantly, what was left of Colin's detached judgment conceded that in bringing Larry Adderley from England to mount this grand rally the Real Truthers had shown excellent sense. First, there was to be a parade from the Mann Square headquarters, but there was none of the self-conscious foolery of most American parades. There was a seriousness about it reminiscent of church ceremonial.

The leaders wore robes, but not gaudy with gold like those of adepts in the other world. Their garb was of plain dark blue, embroidered only with a stylized human figure in white on the left breast, over the heart. They carried large closed books resembling Bibles, and their faces were sober and intent. From the crowd came an occasional mocking laugh, but those were few, and soon died away.

Next came equally serious members of the rank and file of the cult in their Sunday best. These were the ones who made Colin saddest, for among them were many couples in their thirties walking with their children, and their faces were eloquent of calm ecstasy.

Behind them again followed delegates from abroad, each party headed by a blue and gold banner stating no more than the name of the country. The simplicity was impressive; onlookers began to crane their necks or jump up and down to read the name on the next banner.

There was no band marching with them; the accompanying music came from loudspeakers mounted on trees and lampposts, ingeniously timed so that the maximum volume kept pace with the head of the procession.

Altogether there were about fifteen hundred in the parade. The leaders reached the steps of the platform and began to ascend, grouping themselves under Larry's direction in a semicircle framed by the arch. He was in his element today, wearing one of the dark blue robes and with his hair newly cut in imitation of the style affected by Yovan and his fellow adepts.

The remainder of the parade was disposed into a compact bunch facing the platform. The police, who had been cordoning off a clear area for the marchers, relaxed and allowed other bystanders to mingle with them.

Colin watched with aching heart, aware of the impact the efficiency of the ritual must be having.

Then, suddenly, he heard Larry's voice from right beside him, and he glanced around. There he stood, confronting Yovan with a look of self-satisfaction.

"Well, what did I tell you? Did you hear anyone laugh? Did you hear anyone making mock?"

"Get out of my way!" was Yovan's amazing retort.

Larry took a pace back, face falling. "What did you say?"

"Move aside! For all your boasting, we're behind schedule!"

"Now just a moment!" Larry was flushing scarlet. "We're about four minutes off, and that's damned good going for something on this scale! Now there's the invocatory litany to read, and—"

"Then go and read it quietly in a corner somewhere!" Yovan hissed, and deliberately turned his back on Larry to say something in his own language to the fat adept.

As startled as Larry, Colin looked about him. Clearly something was not going according to plan. Nothing was happening for the moment; much more of this and the crowd would grow restless. At the front of the platform the senior cult members were shifting from foot to foot as though nervous.

He turned his attention to his fellow captives. Kolok was no longer lost in a trance of misery. He was glancing alertly from side to side. Vanessa, too, had obviously sensed the change in the situation, and Colin's heart leapt. Dared they hope that the vaunted Real Truth rally was about to dissolve in ignominious fiasco? Could Ishimu, or someone unknown, have struck a blow on their behalf?

But in the same instant there was a sound like the breaking of a violin string, and Yovan's face showed visible relief. He had been sweating; now he wiped his forehead with the sleeve of his robe and started to shoulder his way to the front of the platform.

Larry, infuriated at the abandonment of his cherished ritual, clawed at his arm demanding to know what was going on, and Yovan brushed him aside.

"Do you think you can make Telthis wait out your rigmarole?" he rasped. "Telthis does what he chooses when he chooses! Let me *go!*"

With a violent push he freed himself from Larry's clutch. Seizing a microphone from one of the astonished local cultists, he drew a deep breath.

"He comes! He comes! Witness the advent of the Perfect Man! Bow at his feet, or he will strike you dead with the power of his mind!"

"What the *hell?*" said a single deep voice, loud enough to be heard above the rustle and murmur of the crowd. But nobody else echoed the question. By now everyone was staring up at the arch. Turning his head, Colin saw what had riveted their attention.

Between the pillars, at first too faint and too like the blue of the sky to be detected from ground level, but now distinct and opaque, a mist had gathered. This great triumphal arch was serving to frame a gateway into the other world.

Uncertain how to respond, the crowd was quiet. The Real Truthers were overawed, perhaps dismayed, at this literal interpretation of their creed. The casual watchers were allowing themselves to be impressed by a clever trick. This was better than the regular run of preachy religious meetings, anyhow. Free entertainment was not to be gainsaid.

And tomorrow? If they lived, doubtless they, too, would go willingly to seek the balm of illusory omnipotence, to stare at the whirling spirals that banished doubt and persuaded their dupes that they were masters of the cosmos. Telthis might have to fight, but his victory seemed foregone.

Colin cursed the drug still shackling his mind. He wanted to hate Telthis with the force that, Kolok had claimed, was great enough to withstand even *trnak*. But his whole brain was clouded. There was no fury to call on, only hollow bottomless despair.

But—and the realization broke in on him with the dazzling brilliance of lightning—all of a sudden no one was paying him or Vanessa any attention. Everyone was staring at the arch. Almost before he had conceived the intention, he was on his feet and catching at Vanessa's hand and dragging her after him toward the steps that led to the ground. Larry's plan had called for a robed figure to take station on every tread; with the appearance of the blue mist, however, the cultists had moved to jostle for a better view, and no one hindered them as they scrambled down.

"What about Kolok?" Vanessa cried.

"Too late!" Colin shouted, and thrust between two fat strangers, who uttered mild complaints. "If he could have done anything, he would have—"

Suddenly there was a shriek, and they whirled to see what was happening.

The mist had disgorged its first intruders from the other world. Armed soldiers in ranks of four had stormed into view, cudgels swinging, and sudden panic had overcome the dignitaries of the Real Truth awaiting their messiah. More shrieks followed as they rushed for the steps, and then a scream as one stout man lost his footing and fell down, to be trampled on by others just as frantic.

The alarm spread to the crowd, and fear scented the hot city air. It was no longer Colin and Vanessa only who were eager to leave the square but—in a matter of seconds—hundreds of people who had decided it might be safer somewhere else. Pushing the opposite way, trying to reach the platform, police shoved and cursed in response to orders bawled over a loudspeaker.

Having cleared the platform, the soldiers lowered their cudgels and formed up in a sort of honor guard, by twos, peering in wonder at the strangeness of the city they had come to until their sergeants commanded them to stand at attention.

Then gold glinted in the blue of the mist, and robed adepts began to appear.

"That's more like it!" a young man said reassuringly within earshot of Colin. "That's what they said would happen."

"I don't care!" a girl answered shrilly. "I'm getting out of here!"

Casting glance after anxious glance behind as he tried to lead Vanessa through the throng, Colin saw that the adepts also had lined up either side of the platform. Did that mean Telthis himself was about to emerge?

Not yet. More soldiers. But this time not a token squad to clear the way; instead, a whole horde of them, marching with blind obedience out of the mist, scarcely pausing as they leapt to the ground and threatened the bystanders with their clubs, driving them back. The crowd broke at last, and Colin and Vanessa found themselves being swept along in a river of terrified humanity.

How long before some scared policeman fired the first shot and loosed the wrath of the adepts on them all?

"Hear ye! Hear ye! Hear ye!"

A sudden shout—Yovan's voice again. That must be from Larry's script; it was the ancient English town crier's call. It was so unexpected, it momentarily slowed the panicking crowd.

"He comes, Telthis, your master, lord of two worlds and the Perfect Man!"

"Ohh . . . !" Vanessa gasped, pressing close at Colin's side.

Yes, there he was. Arrogantly striding forward in his golden robe, surveying with greedy eyes the subjects he meant to add to the millions he had already enslaved. The adepts bowed, the soldiers saluted with their cudgels and swords, but the noise from the crowd was not of adoration.

It was compounded of naked terror.

"Let's keep moving!" Colin husked. "So long as we're not actually trapped—"

But Vanessa hadn't heard. Wild-eyed, she pointed at the arch.

"Look! On the steps, going up—Colin, it's Larry!"

Indeed, there he was, rushing the steps heedless of a soldier at his back who was trying to drag him down: Larry, maddened at the ruination of the ritual he had devised with such care and forethought, apparently intent on upbraiding Telthis to his face.

Not understanding what he was doing but admiring his defiance and perhaps ashamed of their own flight, the crowd hesitated. There was an instant of quiet into which Larry hurled a single blazing insult at the top of his voice.

"Perfect Man or no Perfect bloody Man, you're a *bastard!*"

Colin almost shut his eyes, expecting that Telthis would on the instant burn Larry alive or pitch him headlong to the ground and make him tear his own body to bits. Instead, two brawny soldiers closed on him, and he fought back frantically until—

Vanessa's hand clenched painfully on his.

A cudgel had risen high and come down with brutal violence, splitting Larry's skull as a spoon breaks an egg. Blood spattered the soldiers; unconcerned, they heaved his body over the edge of the platform with as little ceremony as men emptying a sack of coal.

"Murderers!" yelled a shrill voice, and the mood of the crowd changed magically. There was something so monumentally loathsome about that casual killing that it wiped away all thought of fear.

"Got a knife?" Colin heard one youth snap, and the reply came prompt from his neighbor.

"God damn, this banjo will make a club!"

"Who are they?"

"Who cares? You saw what they did!"

"Colin, they'll be mowed down!" Vanessa whispered.

"Of course they will! The moment the adepts strike back—!"

Colin bit his lip, torn between retreat and the urge to join the melee now developing around the platform.

"Why haven't they struck already?" Vanessa demanded.

Colin hesitated. "I—I don't know. But . . ."

Shading his eyes, he stared toward the arch, trying to make out whether more invaders were coming through the blue mist. Around the platform a violent fight had broken out; he saw a sword blade rise, sprinkling blood from its tip. Telthis was still there, framed by the arch, face like thunder—and the platform was *rocking*.

"They're pulling it down!" Vanessa shouted. "And Telthis still hasn't stopped them! Colin, the miracle's happened!"

"But how?" Colin countered, scarcely able to let himself believe what he could see. "What's Telthis doing?"

"Losing his temper!" Vanessa said, and laughed.

Yes, that was what it looked like. Telthis was stamping up and down yelling unheeded orders, waving his arms like a madman as the platform swayed to the tugs of the crowd. What had become of the invading soldiers?

There was one of them, limp as a doll, being hoisted over the heads of the attackers and passed hand to hand to the accompaniment of a chant of triumph. A black youth in a red shirt had possessed himself of a sword and was climbing on a friend's back to slash at the proud banners draping the platform. As each fell away, a fresh roar of delight rang out.

"He's beaten!" Colin said, and rubbed his eyes incredulously. "He's trying to run away!"

Telthis had turned his back on his new world. He had run toward the blue mist inside the arch—and escaped to where he came from?

No!

For, unmistakably even at this distance, when he reached the far side of the platform, he had not vanished into nowhere —but simply fallen headlong, and a surge of furious attackers had pounced on him.

"The blue mist!" Colin exclaimed. "It's gone!"

"There goes the platform!" Vanessa cried as the sound of cracking wood reached their ears and the last of the Real Truth banners was dragged down. And then: "Colin! What's that on the arch? Clinging to a ledge! Do you see?"

Something yellow, like a gigantic spider, swinging along the stone coping just below the top.

Ishimu!

Into the hubbub broke a new sound: the clamor of police sirens. Fire trucks, with their high-pressure hoses at the ready, screeched down Fifth Avenue and braked, swerving to left and right. Paddywagons joined them, their doors opening to reveal police in gasmasks who advanced into the square hurling teargas grenades. With gas, and water, and the unrealized threat of their guns, they cleared the crowd away and snapped handcuffs on the bewildered, terrified invaders, while Ishimu clung to his high vantage point and gloried in the downfall of the tyrant he had hated so.

XV

Thanks to Ishimu, Colin and Vanessa managed to evade the general clearance of the square. Choking, because the gas was fierce, they sought out a police sergeant and drew his attention to the yellow figure on the arch.

"That's a kid?" the sergeant said incredulously. "What's he doing—playing Tarzan?" And then, taking a second look: "Hey, he ain't got no legs!"

"That's right," Vanessa said. "He's a cripple. He's never walked."

"Christ! How did he get up there?"

"Does it matter?" Colin countered. "The thing is to get him down!" And, hastily improvising, he added, "He's a war victim, you know. Vietnamese. A good kid, but after what he went through, sort of—uh—crazy sometimes . . ."

The sergeant rubbed his chin and gave a sigh. "Yeah, that figures. Okay, let's see if the fire department can lay on a hook-and-ladder wagon."

Which, after a long delay owing to the people now packed in all the streets leading from the square, half-blind and coughing their guts out from the gas, finally arrived. The fire chief who had radioed for it swore at Ishimu, cockily waving.

"As though we don't have enough to do! I'll give that kid a piece of my mind when we get him down!"

"But he is only a child," Vanessa pleaded. "And he is crippled . . ." She glanced at Colin, who nodded, knowing what was in her mind. Here in this world that had forbidden even Telthis to exercise his supernormal powers, he was going to be even more crippled than before.

"We'll make sure he never does anything like this again," Vanessa insisted. "There's no need for you to concern yourself with him. Like you said, you have more than enough to do—and I must say, you know, you did a marvelous job with your hoses, calming the crowd. I was so afraid someone would have to start shooting, but . . ."

She beamed dazzlingly at the fire chief. A little syrup, a little butter, and the problem was solved. They were allowed, without interference, to carry away the limp but happy Ishimu from the surviving dregs of the crisis, and on the south edge of the square they sat him down on a bench and plied him with the questions that could wait no longer for an answer.

"What are you doing on this side?" Vanessa demanded.

"I wanted to be here when Telthis failed," the boy answered simply.

"How did you know he was going to?" Colin snapped. "Did you—?"

A shadow passed over Ishimu's face, and he held up one thin hand.

"I have a message to give you from Kolok, which will make everything clear."

"Kolok!" Colin started, and Vanessa twisted around, staring toward the arch where the police were still trying to make sense of the arrival of the invaders, weirdly clad and illegally armed and incapable of making themselves understood. By now, ambulances were rolling up; Telthis was likely to be committed to a mental hospital, in that case, and Colin wanted to laugh aloud with joy and relief.

"It's no good looking for him," Ishimu murmured. "You will not see him again. Listen, and I will repeat the message he implanted in my mind."

His voice changed and deepened, as though an echo of Kolok's own had blended with it.

"My friends, you would not have been human had you not wondered why Telthis trusted me so long, permitted me so much freedom—as freedom is measured in my world—and chose me before all his other adepts to make the first exploration through the barrier. The reason is simple. I am his brother. And in his twisted way, perhaps he loved me, as much as a man of his stamp can love at all.

"Thank you for not making me tell you this before. And thank you, too, for not asking why I made no move to help you escape the trap that Yovan set us. I had, as you will learn, another inspiration. If you ever hear this message, you will be aware that I did finally succeed.

"Where I have gone it makes no difference what anyone thinks or says about me. Nonetheless, think well of me sometimes, if you can . . ."

The words died away.

"What has he done?" Colin said, and realization dawned even as he spoke.

"He told you that we had looked into the future and saw that I—*stopped*," Ishimu said. "He did not tell you the same was true of himself. He assumed, of course, that he must meet Telthis face to face in a final battle, and at best he and his brother would both be destroyed. He did not know until the last moment that the truth was otherwise. Myself, I was aware

170

—though out of kindness I did not tell him—that my stopping was to be as you see: permanent exile from my home world. That is the fortune he would have chosen for himself, had he been free. But he was not.

"You saw the blue mist vanish, there between the pillars of the arch?"

"Yes!"

"That was one second after Kolok took his guards by surprise and ran through it into the other world."

"He became *trnak*," Colin said slowly.

"Yes, he did. He is the greatest adept who has ever done so. For no one can tell how far around this spot—a hundred miles, perhaps a thousand—the barrier between the worlds is locked in stasis. Had I your powers, and mine, and Telthis's combined, that could not break it. And he timed the deed so that he trapped Telthis here, together with scores of other adepts loyal to him.

"Back there, I predict chaos. Power will descend to weaklings who will glory in the chance to imitate the behavior of those more talented than they, but they have learned only the viciousness, not the skills, of their departed masters. Factions will develop. There will be wars. The rulers will further weaken themselves. Eventually they may bring about their own downfall; let us hope so, for in that event the race of man can resume the slow upward climb which was halted ten thousand years ago."

"But if you're wrong," Vanessa said, "won't someone else try and breach the barrier—on the other side of the world, perhaps?"

"What would it profit them to repeat Telthis's fatal mistake?" Ishimu said, turning his blind gaze. "Colin understands, I think."

"Yes, I believe I do," Colin confirmed. "You said just now that even if you had our powers you could not break the *trnak* stasis Kolok set up. But he had to return to your side to create it!"

Vanessa's mouth rounded into an O. Ishimu dipped his overlarge head in a sketch for a nod, and his thin mouth curved into a faint smile.

"Indeed. Just as certain devices from your world cannot operate in mine, so certain powers from my world cannot be used in yours. You yourself overcame *trnak* projected by adepts Telthis had personally chosen and brought yourself, Vanessa, and Kolok across the barrier in face of all opposition." Ishimu shivered slightly. "Such power is awe-inspiring, and you never guessed you had it! For here it simply does not work, any more than Telthis's."

Over his head, Colin's eyes met Vanessa's, and he could tell that she was thinking, as he was: *But in that case we would not have to fear what our children might become* . . .

Time enough for that later. They were still, in all the senses that counted, total strangers. But he was whole enough at least to contemplate plans for the future again, free of the suspicion that he was at risk of mental breakdown. There would be no more movement without anything to move at the corner of his eye, no more tampering by Telthis's agents.

He said, "Well, if Kolok was right to say that the universe is a figment of the human mind, it follows that on this side we decline to permit that sort of unbridled power. It does make sense. But . . ." He hesitated, then forced himself to utter the painful truth.

"But it also means, Ishimu, that you are going to be a worse cripple than ever. After so long, I doubt that any doctor, even here, can do much to help you."

Ishimu's mouth quirked. "Did I not recognize you from the top of the arch?" he countered. "Though I say it myself, my talents are unmatched even by Telthis! I've lost many of them —I shall never again be able to float through the air, for example. But I have perceptions that compensate for my blindness. And what is most important, my mind has been set free from fearful fetters. Without Kolok's help I might well have lost my mind. You cannot imagine how the temple teachers policed the thoughts of us apprentices, hoping to batter us into perfect loyalty. Had I let slip one hint of my hatred for Telthis, I should instantly have been cast aside, as being fit only to generate *trnak!*"

And he finished in a tone that mingled joy and sadness inextricably: "Best of all, even though I can bring some of my talents into this world—which Telthis could not—I know that this will cause no harm. Thanks to the way my mother broke my body, there is one part of growing up I shall never know. There will be no inheritors of my power . . ."

There was a long terrible pause. He ended it by putting his thin hands in theirs, smiling.

"Are you not going to introduce me to this strange world? There is much to learn, and I had better make an early start."

Colin, with a nod, rose and gathered the fragile body in his arms. Vanessa at his side, he walked slowly away from the scene of the downfall of the most savage tyrant even that savage species man had contrived to spawn.

- [ ] **THE STONE THAT NEVER CAME DOWN** by John Brunner. There was a forbidden cure for what ailed the world. (#UY1150—$1.25)

- [ ] **POLYMATH** by John Brunner. They trained him as a planet-leader—but for the wrong planet! (#UQ1089—95¢)

- [ ] **THE 1974 ANNUAL WORLD'S BEST SF.** The authentic "World's Best" selection of the year, featuring **Sheckley, Ellison, Eklund, Pohl,** etc. (#UY1109—$1.25)

- [ ] **THE 1973 ANNUAL WORLD'S BEST SF.** This best of the year selection includes **Poul Anderson, Clifford Simak, Tiptree,** and many more. (#UQ1053—95¢)

- [ ] **THE YEAR'S BEST HORROR STORIES: SERIES II.** By popular demand, a new selection of this unique anthology. (#UY1119—$1.25)

- [ ] **CAN YOU FEEL ANYTHING WHEN I DO THIS?** by Robert Sheckley. Marks the return of Sheckley to the ranks of sf-fantasy short story masters. (#UQ1106—95¢)

DAW BOOKS are represented by the publishers of Signet and Mentor Books, THE NEW AMERICAN LIBRARY, INC.

THE NEW AMERICAN LIBRARY, INC.,
P.O. Box 999, Bergenfield, New Jersey 07621

Please send me the DAW BOOKS I have checked above. I am enclosing $_____ (check or money order—no currency or C.O.D.'s). Please include the list price plus 25¢ a copy to cover mailing costs.

Name_____

Address_____

City_____ State_____ Zip Code_____
Please allow at least 3 weeks for delivery

- ☐ **THE BOOK OF BRIAN ALDISS** by Brian W. Aldiss. A new and wonderful collection of his latest science fiction and fantasy masterpieces. (#UQ1029—95¢)

- ☐ **THE BOOK OF PHILIP K. DICK** by Philip K. Dick. A new treasury of the author's most unusual science fiction. (#UQ1044—95¢)

- ☐ **THE BOOK OF GORDON DICKSON** by Gordon R. Dickson. By the author of **Tactics of Mistake** and **Sleepwalker's World**. (#UQ1055—95¢)

- ☐ **THE BOOK OF PHILIP JOSÉ FARMER** by Philip José Farmer. A selection of the author's best in all branches of science fiction, including the facts about Lord Greystroke and Kilgore Trout! (#UQ1063—95¢)

- ☐ **THE BOOK OF FRANK HERBERT** by Frank Herbert. Ten mind-tingling tales by the author of DUNE. (#UQ1039—95¢)

- ☐ **THE BOOK OF FRITZ LEIBER** by Fritz Leiber. Twenty pieces that cover all of Leiber's literary terrain. (#UQ1091—95¢)

- ☐ **THE BOOK OF VAN VOGT** by A. E. van Vogt. A brand new collection of original and never-before anthologized novelettes and tales by this leading SF writer. (#UQ1004—95¢)

DAW BOOKS are represented by the publishers of Signet and Mentor Books, THE NEW AMERICAN LIBRARY, INC.

THE NEW AMERICAN LIBRARY, INC.,
P.O. Box 999, Bergenfield, New Jersey 07621

Please send me the DAW BOOKS I have checked above. I am enclosing
$_____(check or money order—no currency or C.O.D.'s).
Please include the list price plus 25¢ a copy to cover mailing costs.

Name_____

Address_____

City_____State_____Zip Code_____
Please allow at least 3 weeks for delivery

- [ ] **HADON OF ANCIENT OPAR** by Philip José Farmer. An epic action-adventure in Atlantean Africa—in the great Burroughs tradition. Fully illustrated. (#UY1107—$1.25)

- [ ] **A QUEST FOR SIMBILIS** by Michael Shea. Through the weird world of the Dying Earth they sought for justice. (#UQ1092—95¢)

- [ ] **HUNTERS OF GOR** by John Norman. The eighth novel of the fabulous saga of Tarl Cabot on Earth's orbital twin. (#UW1102—$1.50)

- [ ] **THE BURROWERS BENEATH** by Brian Lumley. A Lovecraftian novel of the men who dared disturb the Earth's subterranean masters. (#UQ1096—95¢)

- [ ] **MINDSHIP** by Gerald Conway. The different way of space flight required a mental cork for a cosmic bottle. (#UQ1095—95¢)

- [ ] **MIDSUMMER CENTURY** by James Blish. Thrust into the twilight of mankind, he shared a body with an enemy. (#UQ1094—95¢)

- [ ] **HOW ARE THE MIGHTY FALLEN** by Thomas Burnett Swann. A fantasy novel of the prehumans and the rise of an exalted legend. (#UQ1100—95¢)

DAW BOOKS are represented by the publishers of Signet and Mentor Books, THE NEW AMERICAN LIBRARY, INC.

THE NEW AMERICAN LIBRARY, INC.,
P.O. Box 999, Bergenfield, New Jersey 07621

Please send me the DAW BOOKS I have checked above. I am enclosing $_____(check or money order—no currency or C.O.D.'s). Please include the list price plus 25¢ a copy to cover mailing costs.

Name_____

Address_____

City_____State_____Zip Code_____

Please allow at least 3 weeks for delivery

Presenting the international science fiction spectrum:

☐ **THE ORCHID CAGE** by Herbert W. Franke. The problem of robots and intelligence as confronted by Germany's master of hard-core science fiction. (#UQ1082—95¢)

☐ **GAMES PSYBORGS PLAY** by Pierre Barbet. They made a whole world their arena and a whole race their pawns. (#UQ1087—95¢)

☐ **THE OVERLORDS OF WAR** by Gerard Klein. Translated by John Brunner, this novel of cosmic war and the search for true peace is an sf masterpiece. (#UQ1099—95¢)

☐ **THE MIND NET** by Herbert W. Franke. Within the network, all things were possible and none were permissible . . . (#UQ1136—95¢)

☐ **BERNHARD THE CONQUEROR** by Sam J. Lundwall. A tour-de-force by Sweden's science fiction expert—the novel of a 20,000-mile-long spaceship! (#UQ1058—95¢)

☐ **STARMASTERS' GAMBIT** by Gerard Klein. Games players of the cosmos—an interstellar adventure equal to the best. (#UQ1068—95¢)

DAW BOOKS are represented by the publishers of Signet and Mentor Books, THE NEW AMERICAN LIBRARY, INC.

THE NEW AMERICAN LIBRARY, INC.,
P.O. Box 999, Bergenfield, New Jersey 07621

Please send me the DAW BOOKS I have checked above. I am enclosing $_____(check or money order—no currency or C.O.D.'s). Please include the list price plus 25¢ a copy to cover mailing costs.

Name_____

Address_____

City_____ State_____ Zip Code_____

Please allow at least 3 weeks for delivery

WAS THIS THE EARTH OF ELSEWHEN?

Slowly, the picture of the world grew to completion. In every corner of the planet where the adepts held sway—which meant on four continents, only Australia having failed to tempt them—the commoners lived and died, perhaps without travelling more than a day's walk from home in their entire lifetime.

Draft animals pulled what vehicles they boasted: camels here, llamas there, horses in another place, and for the most part oxen. A few fishing communities owned boats, a few trading rafts plied the larger rivers. But there were no ships. When the adepts could cross oceans by an act of will, what need of them? Better to exploit the sea as a natural prison-wall, shut in the bodies as well as the minds of the common people.

This must not happen to my world! Colin thought, but how could he prevent this alternate Earth from happening?

WAS THIS NOT THE WORLD OF THE PERFECT MAN?